HAUNT HUNTER'S GUIDE TO FLORIDA

JOYCE ELSON MOORE

Pineapple Press, Inc
Sarasota, Florida

Inquiries should be addressed to:
Pineapple Press, Inc.
P.O. Box 3889
Sarasota, Florida 34230
www.pineapplepress.com

Library of Congress Cataloging-in-Publication Data

Moore, Joyce Elson, 1934–
Haunt hunter's guide to Florida / by Joyce Elson Moore.—1st ed.
p. cm.
Includes bibliographical references and index.
ISBN 1-56164-150-2 (alk. paper)
1. Ghosts—Florida. 2. Haunted houses—Florida. 3. Haunted places—Florida. I. Title.
BF1461.M66 1998
133.1'09759—dc21 97-44235

First Edition
10 9 8 7 6 5 4 3

Design by Carol Tornatore
Printed in the United States of America

CONTENTS

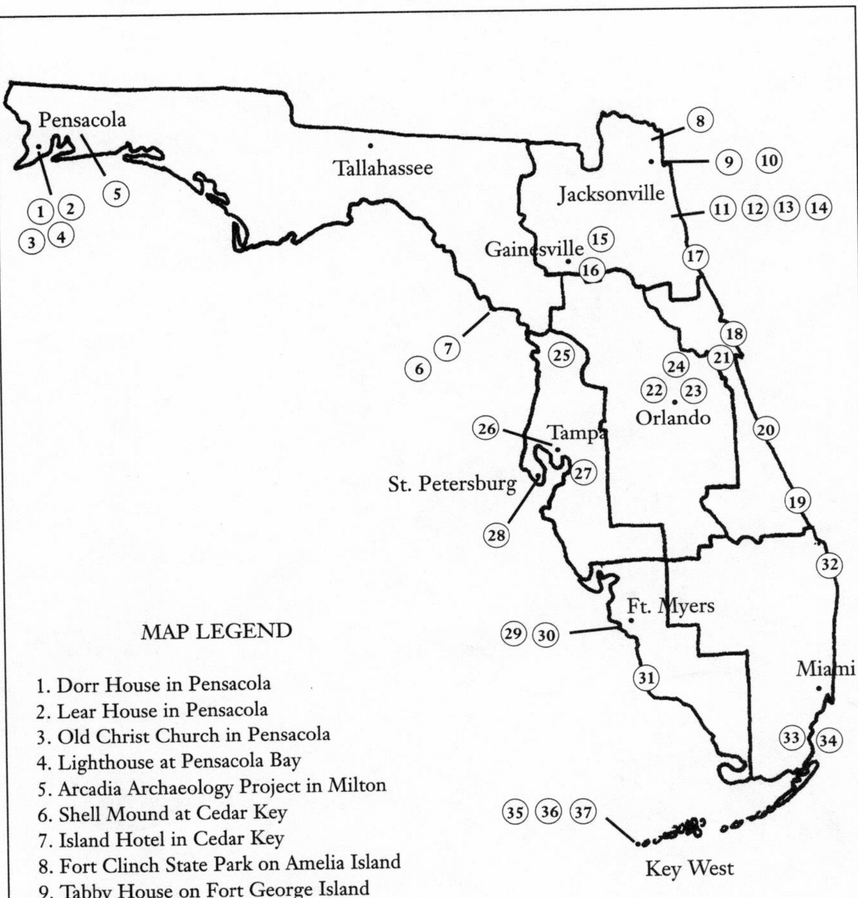

MAP LEGEND

1. Dorr House in Pensacola
2. Lear House in Pensacola
3. Old Christ Church in Pensacola
4. Lighthouse at Pensacola Bay
5. Arcadia Archaeology Project in Milton
6. Shell Mound at Cedar Key
7. Island Hotel in Cedar Key
8. Fort Clinch State Park on Amelia Island
9. Tabby House on Fort George Island
10. Kingsley Plantation on Fort George Island
11. Castillo de San Marcos in St. Augustine
12. St. Francis Inn in St. Augustine
13. 46 Avenida Menendez in St. Augustine
14. Lightkeeper's House in St. Augustine
15. Devil's Millhopper near Gainesville
16. Herlong Mansion in Micanopy
17. Washington Oaks State Gardens near St. Augustine
18. Daytona Playhouse in Daytona Beach
19. Waldo's Mountain in Vero Beach
20. Ashley's in Rockledge
21. Cassadaga near Daytona
22. Maitland Art Center
23. Polasek Galleries in Winter Park
24. Inside-Outside House in Longwood
25. Fort Cooper State Park near Inverness
26. Tampa Theater
27. Center Place in Brandon
28. Johns Pass at Treasure Island
29. Boca Grande Lighthouse on Gasparilla Island
30. Cabbage Key Inn
31. Palm Cottage in Naples
32. Jonathan Dickinson State Park (Trapper Nelson) near Jupiter
33. Coral Castle in Homestead
34. Biltmore Hotel in Coral Gables
35. Artist House in Key West
36. Colours in Key West
37. Fort Zachary Taylor in Key West

INTRODUCTION

In *Florida's folk history libraries*, one can read of apparitions and other hauntings in documents dating back many decades. Florida has an extensive history, and many ghost sites are located in coastal areas where settlers first landed. Numerous ghosts have been reported in older homes, some of which are now listed in the National Register of Historic Places. Some of the more interesting and well-documented haunting sites are in public places such as theaters, parks, and cultural centers—all easily accessible.

The stories have recurring themes—unexplained drafts or sounds, items moved, apparitions seen—but the people who tell of these experiences reflect America's diversity. All those I spoke with—among them a retired Southern matron, a school teacher, park rangers, business people, and many others—were aware that not everyone believes in spirits of the past. Most were reluctant to believe what they saw or heard until the phenomenon became so persistent as to be undeniable. The contributors usually described themselves as having previously been skeptics.

This book is intended to serve as a guide for those who want to experience a different side of Florida than what most visitors see. The locations described here represent a cultural and historic cross-segment of Florida. I have attempted to present the site locations in a way that will allow the visitor to easily enjoy experiencing them. It is my hope that in visiting these sites, the reader comes to know and love Florida for its sometimes unusual past.

The seven sections of the book correspond to regions of the state as shown on the map on page v. Each entry includes a general discussion of the site's history and character; its "haunt history," which often includes extensive excerpts from my interviews with owners or caretakers; and details about how best to experience the site, including nearby attractions and facilities.

The relevance or accuracy of these stories can only be discovered by the individual, as the truth of folklore can only be realized within oneself. I hope you enjoy this tour of Florida's haunt history as much as I have enjoyed compiling it.

REGION ONE

NORTHWEST

DORR HOUSE IN PENSACOLA

The *prominent yellow house* which faces Old Christ Church in Pensacola is known as the Dorr House. During the 1870s and 1880s, this neighborhood was the city's most prestigious residential area. The house is considered to be the best-preserved example of post–Civil War Classical Greek Revival architecture in the area.

Clara Barkley and Eben Walker Dorr married in 1849. Eben's father, Ebenezer Dorr, was the first sheriff of Escambia County when Florida became a state in 1821. As sheriff, he arrested Jonathan Walker for slave stealing. John Greenleaf Whittier immortalized the affair in "The Branded Hand," one of his series of antislavery poems. Eben's grandfather, William, is reported to have ridden with Paul Revere on his famous ride, etching the Dorr name in history. Eben was a partner in Simpson and Company, a large sawmill in Bagdad, Florida, near Pensacola. At his death in 1870, his widow, Clara Barkley Dorr, received $51,195.82 for his interest in the lumber company, a huge amount at that time. In 1871 she bought a lot facing Seville Square and built the house with part of the proceeds. Clara moved into the house with their five children and lived there until 1896.

The house is typical of homes of the prosperous during the 1870s. There is a parlor, a dining room, and a long hall leading to the kitchen. Upstairs there are four rooms and a hall. The high ceilings and the archway between the parlor and dining room reflect typical construction of that time period, and the slate mantels for coal-burning fireplaces are in every room. The Pensacola Heritage Foundation purchased the house in 1964 and began its restoration. The Historic Pensacola Preservation Board, an agency of the state of Florida, purchased it in 1975, and the house is now included in the Historic Pensacola Village walking tour.

HAUNT HISTORY

Many of the guides for the historic walking tour confess to not being comfortable in the house. They have reported seeing shadows or

Dorr House

forms, that, when they turn to look at them directly, disappear. As is common with poltergeists, things are frequently moved about. One guide who gave a demonstration of antique household items to a group left the house as usual for the rest of the tour. Upon returning to the house to get the articles ready for the next tour, she found that the demonstration articles had already been replaced in their original locations. She had been the last person to leave the house, and the only one to return in preparation for the next tour. Another time, when she was alone at the house, she felt someone pulling on her skirt. A neighbor reported hearing the alarm in the house go off. At the time, the power to the alarm had not yet been connected. There is no explanation for these happenings in the Dorr House. Some of the Dorr children died at an early age after moving into the house with their mother. It is speculated that the presences experienced here could be any one of several people, as the Dorr family history is ripe with strong personalities who perhaps hated to leave the lovely house near Seville Square.

VISITING THE SITE

The Historic Village is open from 10:00 A.M. to 4:00 P.M. every Monday through Saturday year-round, and Sundays from Memorial Day to Labor Day. Admission is $5.50 for adults, $4.50 for seniors, and $2.25 for children 4–16 years of age (under 4 admitted free). The tickets are good for two days. The tickets include entry to the T. T. Wentworth State Museum as well as the historic homes. Also included in the ticket prices is admission to the Museum of Commerce, a reconstructed streetscape with a toy store, pharmacy, music shop, hardware store, and print shop. The print shop contains one of the most complete collections of antique presses and type in the entire Southeast. This museum also houses a collection of horse-drawn buggies. The Museum of Industry is a series of exhibits representing the major early industries in Pensacola, including the lumber and railroad industries, among others. Call (850) 444-8905 for more information.

DIRECTIONS

From Garden Street (Hwy. 98), turn south on Palafox to Government. Turn left on Government to Taragona Street, turn right onto Taragona, then left onto Zaragoza Street for your tickets or street parking to view the homes from the exterior.

LEAR HOUSE IN PENSACOLA

The property on which the Lear house now stands, at 214 East Zaragoza Street, changed ownership many times before being purchased by Kate and John Lear, who began construction on the house in 1887. In 1897 it was sold to ship owner Benito Rocheblave and Katherine Elizabeth, his wife. The Rocheblave family lived there until 1912. Although others have owned the house, it is known as the Lear-Rocheblave House. It is considered to be an excellent example of folk Victorian or frame vernacular architecture, identifiable by the irregular floor plan and elaborate roof system. It is a two-story frame house with ornamented porches, noted for the chamfered and bracketed columns. On the second floor, the porches boast a scrollwork balustrade, except for the rear porches, where there are wood railings. The main entrance has a transom and sidelights. It is part of the Historic Pensacola Village tour.

HAUNT HISTORY

During the renovation of the Lear House, a painter working on the project saw a woman in Victorian dress dancing in one of the bedrooms on the second floor. He hastily climbed down his ladder and alerted his fellow workers, who entered the house and went up to the bedroom where the painter had seen the woman. They found no one in the room, but according to the workers, there was a strong odor of perfume in only that room. A former visitor to the house related being shown around the house when she visited the family, but never being shown this room, which remained closed during her visit.

When students from the University of West Florida were conducting an archaeological dig at the Old Christ Church, their equipment and artifacts were stored in the Lear House. Among these were

Lear House

coffins containing skeletons of the rectors, which had been excavated. The remains were stored in the house before being sent to Florida State University to be identified and after they were returned to the correct coffins to be reburied. The archaeologists left one evening, after carefully placing all the bones in the correct order. The next morning, they found the door locked as they had left it, but the bones in each of the boxes had been moved around. There was no evidence that anyone had entered the house after the students locked it for the evening.

Strange things happen in the Lear House, but there is no explanation for them. Who haunts this old house is unknown. We only know it is a female apparition who is seen and felt around the house. Who she is remains a mystery. Possibly it is a former owner, but there is no explanation for her continued presence in this house.

VISITING THE SITE

This historic house, like the Dorr House, is on the tour of Historic Pensacola Village. For hours and fees, see the information listed for the Dorr House (p. 5). After a day spent enjoying the many faces of Pensacola, plan to dine at The Oyster Bar on North Navy Boulevard. It's recommended by locals, and for good reason: The seafood is the best. Phone (850) 455-3925.

OLD CHRIST CHURCH IN PENSACOLA

On *a warm June day* in 1827, a group of citizens gathered in Pensacola to determine the feasibility of establishing a Protestant church. Encouraged by the interest of those attending, they agreed to petition the Territorial Legislature for incorporation, and set in motion plans to build a church. The vestry (lay people who were the governing body for the church) bought the land on which the church now stands for four hundred dollars. The building was finished in 1832 at a cost of forty-five hundred dollars. It was built of brick, and on the west wall was a vestry room and study.

Walker Anderson, a parishioner who later became a Chief Justice of the Supreme Court of Florida, wrote that in 1839, Rev. Joseph Saunders, who died at age thirty-nine of yellow fever, was buried beneath the vestry room, just below the spot in which he sat while preparing his sermons. Although there were no official records, it is mentioned in a history of the parish that two other rectors, Rev. Frederick F. Peake and Rev. David D. Flower, were also buried beneath the floor of the church.

Later this vestry room was torn down and the church building was extended twenty feet over that area. This addition created a kind of basement under the old vestry area, which would subsequently become a source of intrigue for historians and archaeologists. Besides being a place of worship, the structure served as a barracks, jail, and hospital for Union soldiers. Later, rumors persisted that the soldiers had vandalized the graves of the three rectors.

In 1988 the Archaeological Institute of the University of West Florida, at the invitation of Dr. Currin, rector of Christ Church, began an archaeological investigation into the whereabouts of the bodies of the three priests, who had all died in their thirties while serving the parishioners at Old Christ Church. The archaeologists and students, headed by Dr. Judith Bense, were anxious to determine if the remains of the three interred priests were still where they had been buried. They also hoped to uncover artifacts that might help reconstruct a part of Pensacola's past.

The two-month search for and recovery of the three rectors is compiled for public reading as The Search for the Lost Rectors: Archaeology and History of Old Christ Church. Gary Powell, a student at the University of West Florida during that year, wrote the first half of the document. It is a project report of the discovery of the partially disturbed remains of the three priests, their identification by a forensic anthropologist from Florida State University, and their subsequent reinterment under the church. It is the reinterment with which we are concerned for the purposes of this book. Descriptions of

Old Christ Church

the procession for the reburial are consistent, with one exception. Gary Powell, a paraplegic young man who, at age fifteen, was paralyzed after being hit by a motorcycle, saw something at the burial that the others were not privileged to see. He includes this in his project report, and consented to talk to me about his experience.

HAUNT HISTORY

When Powell saw the three rectors, he "thought it was strange. For one, they weren't wearing shoes. They were wearing robes and like a scarf around the neck—they call it a stole. The one in the middle was carrying a black book—a leather-covered book embossed with a cross. He was quiet, very solemn, and the other two on each side of him were cross-talking in front of him, just laughing and carrying on, and he seemed to be embarrassed by it. He had a solemn look on his face. I just stared at them. They were stairsteps from one another in height. One had glasses, and one was more heavy-set than the others. They had reddish-colored skin, like you'd think if you touched them it would leave a white mark where your finger was. The two were just carrying on, and when I took my eyes off them to look at the caskets that had been made, identical to the ones they were originally buried in, I lost track of them. I asked the person next to me, 'Where are those three men?' She said, 'What three men?' I said 'Those three.' She said, 'I don't know what you're talking about. I want to watch the ceremony.' And later on I asked someone who they were, and they didn't know what I was talking about. I can describe what they were wearing. I stared at them. I thought they were kind of rude. That day the priest came to our table and told me that priests are buried barefooted. They wear robes and have a stole around their neck, and they are buried with a black prayer book. And the three men were stair-step different in height, which these three men were. I said, 'Gee, I saw them at their own funeral.' The guy who built the caskets saw them, too, as he was making the caskets in his garage."

In the report Gary submitted as a student at the University of West Florida, he described the funeral, including the three men. The description of the funeral by others who were there do not include the three. The sidewalk down which the burial procession took place is beside the church, and overlooked by the Lear House, where the remains were temporarily kept during the research. Only the old church knows the entire truth of what happened here. Possibly the story is just beginning.

VISITING THE SITE

Old Christ Church was used to house the Pensacola Historical Society Museum until September 1966. The church is deeded to the Old Christ Church Foundation, which is entering into a ninety-nine-year lease with the Historic Pensacola Preservation Board, operated under a branch of the Florida Department of State. The old church is being fully restored to its original nineteenth-century condition. Cost of restoration will be $600,000. It will be a centerpiece for the historical district, serving as a community center, and will be available for weddings and cultural events.

DIRECTIONS

Old Christ Church directly faces Seville Square, in the heart of historic downtown Pensacola.

LIGHTHOUSE AT PENSACOLA BAY

T*he gulls look out across* Pensacola Bay, all facing the same way, whether perched or preening. Overhead, planes from the Naval Air Station fly in formation, and the lighthouse stands—a silent guardian of this lovely piece of Florida. It is here that Spanish ships brought pioneers, eager to claim this deep harbor as the Crown's own. Watching barges pushing freighters beside the string of islands, it is easy to imagine pirates and gold, trinkets and treasures, sunken too long ago for recovery. The rich history of the area leaves us to question who has lived here, and why any soul would want to leave. And perhaps this alone tells why the region is ripe with tales of spiritual wanderings and of ghosts of Creek natives, Spanish and English settlers, and missionaries.

The lighthouse at the Naval Air Station is still operative. It stands 191 feet above sea level, and is visible for twenty-seven miles. Established in 1858, it was constructed after continued complaints about the original tower, which stood only thirty feet high and whose light to certain bay areas was obscured by trees. The original light was built roughly sixteen hundred feet to the east of the existing light, near where the present Navy Lodge and Lighthouse Restaurant are located.

Pensacola Bay figured so prominently in the Civil War that historian Canter Brown Jr. is quoted as saying the " war almost began, in fact, at Pensacola rather than at Fort Sumter." Pensacola was the gathering place of Confederate forces from Alabama and Florida after the secession vote. The Union promised not to increase troops in the area, and the two sides were able to operate under an informal truce. However, in May of 1861, the Confederates sank several ships to block the channel between the Gulf of Mexico and Pensacola Bay. In turn, the Union destroyed the town's dry dock and naval repair facilities. An artillery duel in November between the opposing sides damaged the lighthouse, which had been requisitioned for use as a lookout tower for the Confederates. Union forces took Pensacola in May. The town was now almost deserted; the departing Confederates

Lighthouse at NAS, Pensacola

had burned buildings and supplies, but the lighthouse still stood.

In 1863 the lighthouse was again being used for its original purpose, but with a smaller lens. In 1869, a first-order Fresnel lens was reinstalled to guide ships through the harbor. Lightning strikes and a tornado damaged part of the lighthouse and keeper's house, and the Charleston Earthquake of 1886 made "a rumbling, as if people were ascending the steps, making as much noise as possible" (according to "Pensacola Lighthouse History" [see bibliography]). The lighthouse was electrified in 1939 and continued to be manned until 1965.

The keeper's house and connecting buildings form the entrance to the tower. The 178 steps to the tower are steep, and, unlike the St. Augustine lighthouse, there are no landings on which to pause, but the climb is rewarded as one stands at the top.

HAUNT HISTORY

When the lighthouse quarters were open for overnight guests in 1976, some of the guests fled in the middle of the night in terror and would not return for their belongings, says Amond Steele, Vice Captain of Division 1, Coast Guard Auxiliary Flotilla 17, who used to be the tour guide for the lighthouse. Steele relates that Jeremiah Ingraham, who died in 1840, is believed to have been killed by his wife, Michaela, who took over the lighthouse keeper's duties until her own death fifteen years later. Although Ingraham died in the original lighthouse, his ghost is believed to roam the present structure built a short distance away. Unexplained bloodstains were reported in an upstairs bedroom of the keeper's quarters, covered by tile laid during an earlier renovation. In the later renovation, completed in 1995, tile was removed and indeed bloodstains were there. The original pinewood floor revealed the stains as workers removed the felt and vinyl tiles which had lain there since the 1950s. "The stains are definitely blood," said Leo Glenn, a construction supervisor. The stains include one large, dark blotch and several splatters. "We figured there was a bed here in the middle and they fought all the way around the bed," he said. Although there are no official records of a murder having taken place in that room, Dick Callaway, cultural resource manager for the Naval Air Station, believes the stains are blood. However, the U.S. Navy does not intend, as part of its $250,000 renovation of the keeper's quarters, to have the bloodstains scientifically analyzed.

Emmit Hatten, who lived in the lighthouse when his father was keeper, told of how his mother scrubbed the bloodstains to remove them, only to have them repeatedly reappear. Hatten also said he heard human breathing when no one else was around, and his parents heard footsteps on the massive iron staircase at night.

A Navy Recreation Department employee had experiences that have gone unexplained. During his rounds, he noticed that one of the windows about halfway up the lighthouse was open. He climbed the stairs, and closed and locked the window. When he returned to his car, he noticed that the window was again open. He climbed back up, relocked the window, and, returning to his car, saw that it had been opened yet again.

Steele, the former Coast Guard tour guide, has found several doors open that were supposedly secured. When he and his wife were in the lighthouse one time, they heard a heavy iron trap door, at the top of the stairs which allows access to the light room, slam shut. Steele said he went to investigate, and the door was locked. "This is a strange place," Steele was quoted as saying.

During the recent renovations, Callaway recorded several incidents involving workers on the site. One man had a water hose yanked out of his hand. Two others spied a figure in the window of the locked lighthouse. Others told him they felt a sudden chill on warm days and caught whiffs of pipe tobacco. "Every incident that I recorded had two or more people to witness it," Callaway offered. The construction crew also reported that a locked door at the back of the keeper's quarters kept swinging open at night.

Locals believe there are three separate ghosts who haunt the Pensacola lighthouse. A psychologist who stayed at the lighthouse several years ago confirmed the existence of ghosts there. Two of the ghosts are keepers who died a natural death at the lighthouse, and the third is the ghost of Ingraham, the keeper in the original tower.

VISITING THE SITE

Very near the lighthouse is the National Museum of Naval Aviation. It is one of the world's largest air and space museums displaying historical warbirds. The first airplane to cross the Atlantic is housed here. Lighthouse tours are on Sundays only, 12:00 noon to 5:00 P.M. from Memorial Day to Labor Day. Special arrangements can sometimes be made for groups by calling (850) 455-2354. The Navy Lodge is a wonderful place to stay if you are eligible to use it (active or retired military, reservists, Department of Defense employees, and their families). Rooms are spacious, and some face the beach. All rooms are just a short walk to the beach, down a brick paved walkway, complete with showers to wash the Florida sand from your feet before returning to the lodge.

DIRECTIONS

The lighthouse may be accessed by entering the back gate on Radford Road. Currently, there is an open-gate policy at the Naval Air Station.

ARCADIA ARCHAEOLOGY PROJECT IN MILTON

After years of abandonment, the first and largest water-powered industrial complex in Florida has come to the attention of historians and archaeologists. Although the mystery lay buried by a century of soil and water, the University of West Florida Archaeology Institute determined that information about this large-scale operation might be uncovered at the Arcadia dig, and they, together with the Santa Rosa Historical Society, exposed and documented enough remains to interpret the site.

We now know that this complex played a pivotal role in the development of northwest Florida. There were mills, shops, a mule-drawn railroad, and a sixteen-mile log flume to move the virgin lumber cut down in the surrounding area. A water-powered sawmill had planing machines, lathes, and a grist mill.

The land was first granted to Juan de la Rua in 1817. He may have begun construction of a dam. However, his efforts were thwarted by hostile Indians who roamed the area, and in 1828 he sold the

Museum at Arcadia Archaeological Project

property to Joseph Forsyth. Forsyth seriously began construction of a dam and sawmill, bringing Ezekial and Andrew Simpson in as partners. Forsyth sold the northeast quarter of Arcadia to Timothy Twitchell, who excavated a flume to connect his newly dammed creek to Arcadia. When the lumber from the pine forests was transported to the flume and carried to the Arcadia mill pond, it was separated into groups—the yellow pine went to the Forsyth-Simpson mills, and the cypress and juniper floated down to Twitchell's mills.

In the 1830s, steam power came to northwest Florida. No longer was it necessary to locate mills on streams for water power, so Forsyth and Simpson moved their lumber mills to Bagdad. But they seemed reluctant to leave their beloved water-powered complex, so they built the Arcadia Manufacturing Company, which contained a cotton textile factory. By 1853, their mill was the largest and most successful textile factory in Florida, and it was operated by female slaves. A few months after Forsyth's death, at age fifty-three, the textile mill burned. Except for a small skirmish between Union and Confederate troops, the industrial complex was abandoned for 109 years. Warren Weekes, a local historian, rediscovered the mill site in 1964. It was placed on the National Register of Historic Places.

"The timber was the gold the Spaniards had been looking for," Mr. Weekes explained. "Our gold stood out here ten to fifteen feet around and one hundred twenty feet high. And they said 'How can we get this to Europe?' So they came up with an idea: 'Let's build a big dam, raise up a mill pond, put box culverts through the dam, and let the water spill on a wheel. That will be our source of energy. We'll cut down these big trees and square them and put them on ships and send them to the Mediterranean.' The European states didn't have any timber. They still don't."

During the tour, he showed me an electrified version of a saw. "In 1840, Disston invented a round saw, but how did they do it before 1840? This is my idea." Then he showed me heart pine held together with juniper pegs. He explained that the names Sawyer and Pit(t)man came from the two men who handled the lumber. The sawyer was up above, feeding the lumber into the saw, and the pit man was down below—thus the names.

HAUNT HISTORY

"You can hear footsteps, as if I were walking out there and you knew it. I have been to that door, I'd say—in five years—maybe a thousand times, because I knew someone was walking on the porch," explained Mr. Weekes. He continued, saying that when he sat at the table working, or perhaps reading, he could feel the floor vibrating with the steps of the unknown presence. One of the ghosts is Forsyth, he offered, showing me a picture clearly labeled "Joseph Forsyth, 1802-1855." He also believes Simpson is one of the ghosts. Weekes said he could hear voices sometimes when he was working in the front part of the museum, but couldn't hear what they were saying. He said they didn't bother him, and he isn't worried about the two partners being around. He believes they came back to stay near their sawmill, especially since there was renewed interest and digging around for artifacts.

VISITING THE SITE

Mr. Weekes, who is largely responsible for the renewed interest in the site, is now the museum curator and site manager. He gives tours by appointment. Call (850) 626-4433. The museum holds artifacts discovered on the site, and Mr. Weekes brings the complex to life again as he explains the exhibits and tools there. With the grinding of the saw in the background, one almost expects to see Forsyth and Simpson checking on their investment.

DIRECTIONS

Call for a tour of the museum (850) 623-3762. Arcadia is just off US 90, south of Milton. Take Exit 6 off I-10 (Avalon/Milton exit). At first stoplight, turn left onto Hwy. 90. Turn right on Anna Simpson, the second road past the Monsanto Employees Credit Union sign. Go one-half mile on this road to a "T"; turn left onto Mill Pond Lane. Museum is on the left and has a red, white, and blue mailbox.

SHELL MOUND AT CEDAR KEY

Just where Florida begins stretching her western coastline toward the Panhandle lies a group of islands in the Gulf. One of these, Cedar Key, is easily accessible by bridges that span the channels between the key and the mainland. Still predominantly a fishing village, Cedar Key has nevertheless attracted artists and shopkeepers who shun the busier lifestyle of central and lower Florida. Just northeast of Cedar Key lies the Lower Suwannee National Wildlife Refuge, a fifty-one-thousand-acre refuge established in 1977 with the objective of preserving the Suwannee River delta and estuary ecosystem. A huge shell mound, thousands of years old, lies in this refuge.

Years of coastal hurricanes have altered the land, and the twelve-foot-deep hole from which Annie Simpson's ghost rose has mellowed into pockets of shallow holes around the mound. But the mound itself still rises above the .3-mile trail that circles around the base. It is clearly marked as the Shell Mound Trail, and offers a superb view of the estuary below. A sturdy bench at the overlook provides the wildlife photographer a perfect spot to watch the wading birds that feed there as the tides change.

Trail to Cedar Key Shell Mound

HAUNT HISTORY

The ghost, whom many local fishermen have seen, is that of a beautiful girl with long dark hair, dressed in a light-colored blouse and a dark skirt. Her wolfhound-type dog is always with her. Before the turn of the century, pirates buried treasure near the shell mound, and Annie Simpson and her dog happened to come upon them accidentally. The pirates killed her and the dog, guaranteeing that she would never tell what she had seen. Locals say that people "with no greed in their hearts can dig that treasure up. It's in quicklime. Ask her (Annie) what she wants; she'll talk to you."

In November of 1995, Anna Ray Roberts sat in her kitchen telling me of her experiences with Annie Simpson's ghost. "My ex-husband and I were oystering for a living back in sixty-nine. We were staying on Garden Island, off of Shell Mound. I had a little fifty-nine Chevrolet. Well, it's so far by water from Shell Mound to Cedar Key, we figured it would be cheaper to take that old car to Shell Mound, take the back seat out of it and the trunk lid off, and we could haul our oysters in it, rather than run the boats into town. A friend of ours,

Denny Gleason, and my husband were going to take the boat to Shell Mound, and I was going to drive that old car up there. It was in the middle of January, and cold. There was a road that went down to Shell Mound and down to the water. I pulled down to the water and faced southwest, so if I heard them come I could flash on the lights. All I heard was the wind blowing, and I was getting cold. Up in the northwest was a big black cloud."

"I got tired of sitting behind the steering wheel, so I turned around and put my arm up on the back, and then I saw this light coming down the lane. I quickly locked all the doors. This light was nine inches around . . . no glow, perfectly round . . . about five feet off the ground. It wasn't bobbing like a headlamp on somebody's cap. It wasn't a lantern. It wasn't a flashlight. It was just moving very slowly. Then it got right to the last rise, and it came to where my car was, and just hung there, suspended in air. Without going up, down, or sideways, it moved over through the trees. Never did come down to where I was. And then the light went out. I never did see it anymore."

"I lived on Front Street across from Janie and Curly Robinson then. Janie and I built crab traps in her living room. I got to telling her what I had seen at Shell Mound. I looked at Janie. She was as white as a sheet. She looked at Curly and he looked at her, and I said 'Did I say something wrong?' She said, 'Tell her, Curly.' He said, 'I don't want to talk about it.' Then she told me that one night she and Curly were out at Shell Mound and their boat was stuck in the mud. Nature called, and she went into the woods. Then she came running out of the woods screaming. It was a full moonlit night; that's why the tide was so low. That woman was right behind her. She had on a long dress, and the same round light for a head. The ghost was about a foot off the ground. She didn't see any body, just the light and the white dress. Pirates killed Annie and her dog, and she travels Shell Mound."

At that point Anna Ray interrupted her talk to offer coffee, and then resumed her story. "There have been jokes made about it, and people thought I was off my rocker, but I know what I saw. Another time we were staying at Garden Island, and we had a little red dog. One night he got to barking and barking. We knew he wasn't barking at another boat, because it was low tide. We always tied our boat to the south end of the island because there was a channel there and we could get out even at low tide. We got up to see what he was barking at, and that ghost woman was sitting on the bow of the boat. We went back to bed. I wasn't about to go out there."

She went on to tell of another time a friend of hers was at Shell Mound waiting for her husband to get back from crabbing. "Her eight-year-old daughter walked toward the woods. Her mother told her to come back, but the little girl said, 'Mama, she wants me.' She just kept walking, saying she had to go. 'She wants me, Mama.' She got up and went after her daughter, and just as she caught her, she saw the woman standing there beckoning with her finger. What she wanted with the little girl, I don't know. Another time they were driving on the path near Shell Mound, and the little girl leaned out of the car window and said, 'There she is . . . the woman and her dog.'"

A treasure hunter from St. Petersburg says that he did indeed find parts of old chests that had fallen apart when someone tried to move them. Metal detectors were used near the mound, and coins have been unearthed. The complete skeleton of a dog was found. Annie Simpson's physical remains were never found, but her spirit remains near the Shell Mound, walking with her dog in the mists that rise from the swampy area below the mound.

VISITING THE SITE

In another part of the Lower Suwannee Refuge is a walking trail leading to the Suwannee River. The boardwalk is a scenic path affording a good view of the river. A sheltered board holds pamphlets about the trail, pictures of the wading birds, and pictures of the bottomland hardwoods and their identifying leaves. A pine needle path, with frequent signposts about the wildlife that lives in the area, extends to the Suwannee River.

Maps of the loop, with walking trails indicated, are available at the parking areas at Shell Mound and at the River Walk. Because this is Florida lowland country, wear insect repellent if you visit during the summer months. Accommodations available in Cedar Key range from a bed and breakfast that keeps bicycles out back for guests' use, to a small twelve-room remodeled Cracker house, where the gulf breeze flutters the curtains at the windows, to a haunted old hotel (see next chapter). After visiting the Lower Suwannee National Wildlife

Refuge, allow another full day for browsing in the galleries and boutiques along the quiet Cedar Key streets. Restaurants with porches overlooking the water offer fresh local seafood daily. Don't miss Sweet Memories, squeezed in between the restaurants, for a taste of freshly made fudge, taffy, and peanut brittle.

DIRECTIONS

From Rt. 19, turn west at Otter Creek onto S.R. 24. Just east of Cedar Key, turn north onto 347. At 326 turn left toward the Shell Mound. After the pavement ends, continue on the gravel road. On the left is the parking area for the Shell Mound. Get a map here showing the layout of the refuge, and it will indicate the location of the other trail, near the Refuge Headquarters, which leads to the Suwannee River.

THE ISLAND HOTEL IN CEDAR KEY

Opening the door into the lobby of the Island Hotel is taking a walk back in time. The dark wood floors, the comfortable old furniture, and the high white baseboards put the visitor in another place, a quieter time, when Florida was still young. One would not be more than mildly surprised to see Bogart and Bacall, or maybe Hemingway, sipping a drink at the cedar-topped bar. Indeed, venerated guests have stayed at the hotel. Pearl S. Buck, Vaughn Monroe, Tennessee Ernie Ford, Myrna Loy, and Richard Boone, among others, have signed the guest log. In an earlier time, Union soldiers probably camped there, as it was one of the few places not burned down in Cedar Key during the Civil War. At the time, it was a general store and was useful to the invading army of soldiers. In 1984, the hotel was placed on the National Register of Historic Places.

Each of the ten rooms is uniquely decorated. Some of the bathrooms have clawfooted tubs, while others have washbasins and showers. All the beds are draped with mosquito netting and piled high with linens. Low-slung chairs invite the visitor to sit awhile, read a book, or just gaze out a window. Visitors can enjoy dinner in the candlelit dining room or on the screened-in side porch. Slowly rotating paddle fans, lush greenery, and a quiet atmosphere tempt one to stay in this peaceful place forever. You won't find any television sets or ringing phones here. There is nothing here but a relaxed ambiance and history so strong that it seems the aged building holds more stories than the old-timers in Cedar Key. Time has left its mark on the Island Hotel and has left ghosts of that history. Their presence is a persistent and comforting phenomenon within its lovely old walls.

HAUNT HISTORY

There are several permanent guests who evidently feel welcome enough to stay around the Island Hotel along with the registered guests and current owners. These "wandering presences" have strong ties to the old place, both historically and spiritually. In 1915, Stan Feinberg, a Florida businessman, bought the Parsons and Hale's General Store and converted the building into the Bay Hotel. Feinberg leased out the hotel, which proved to be disastrous for him. He had difficulty collecting his lease money and had to come to Cedar Key to settle with his tenant. On one of these trips he discovered that an illegal whiskey still was being operated from the attic. He was incensed, and let the leasee know. To placate Feinberg, the man put on a large dinner party that evening, with most of the businessmen in Cedar Key invited. Feinberg ate dinner, retired, and never awoke. Tom Sanders, who owned the Island Hotel from 1992 to 1996, said that a descendant of Feinberg's had told him that Feinberg died in the hotel. "It's common knowledge in the Feinberg family that he was poisoned. I'm convinced that Feinberg is probably one of the ghosts," Sanders said.

Alison Sanders, Tom's wife, described several "appearances" during their ownership. "Bessie, a former owner, is one of the ghosts," she said emphatically. "I think maybe sometimes Bessie sent me messages. Once in a while she locked me out when I was doing a lot of changes. I walked out into the courtyard and couldn't get back in. When we had the upstairs bathrooms re-enameled, it took the man roughly an hour for each room to do both the tub and sink. When he did Bessie's room, it took him three and one-half hours and four coats of enamel, and he was only doing the sink. It was like Bessie was saying, 'Now hang on here a minute.' Whenever we hired a new housekeeper, Bessie started opening and closing doors; she did it just to see if she wanted them (the housekeepers) around." Tom interjected: "I don't think Bessie has ever manifested herself visually, but Bessie was notorious for being very short with people. The hotel has a clientele, people who stay there because of what it is."

Alison continued: "I only know two people who have seen a ghost. But in each case, the only ghost that's been seen was a lady in white. These people said that a lady in white came into their room and sat on the edge of their bed. They asked, 'What are you doing in my room?' and she got up and walked across the room and straight out through the wall. They were one-hundred percent convinced that they had actually seen something. I don't know who she is or why she was back. When an earlier owner held a seance at the hotel, a lady in white appeared, or was referred to at that seance. But I don't know her history."

Bessie and "Gibby" Gibbs owned the hotel from 1946 to 1973. The two were colorful figures around Cedar Key. The hotel bar, with Gibby mixing the drinks, became a popular local gathering place for then-governor Claude Kirk as well as for Hollywood celebrities wanting a place to get away from their high-profile lives. The Gibbses arranged for murals to be painted on the walls of the Neptune Bar, some of which can still be seen. Gibby's health failed, but he continued to be nursed by Bessie in his room at the hotel. His death in 1962 did not preclude his being behind the bar. Bessie put his cremated ashes in an urn, and when asked by a visitor why she had the urn behind the bar, she replied, "Because that's where he was happiest." In truth, Bessie was waiting for high tide so that she could fulfill his wish of having his ashes scattered at sea. Bessie died in 1975 not far from the hotel, in a house she had moved into after selling the hotel.

"A lady checked in after we'd owned the hotel for about two years," Tom said. "The room she stayed in was the one Bessie and Gibby used. She stayed with us for two days, and as she was checking out she said, 'You know, that room is haunted. There were two people whose ghosts are in that room. One of them died a violent death—but not in the hotel—and had a long history with the building. And the other one died earlier—I believe they were a couple, and the other suffered a long illness.' Well, that is Bessie and Gibby Gibbs. They lived up in room twenty-nine. Gibby got cancer and was nursed here. Bessie died a violent death in a house fire. This was before I did the history on it, so unless this woman secretly went out and did a lot of research on it, she couldn't have known." He added that she said there were other ghosts at the front of the hotel from an earlier period. When he asked how she knew this, she showed him a business card. "She had training at Duke University, which had a Division of Parapsychology. Her credentials were pretty good. She didn't seem like a huckster type. She seemed to know what she was talking about."

Tom Sanders concluded, "The only time that I've really felt the presence of something, I had been to the airport that night, and I drove back to the hotel. I got back in the middle of a lightning storm, with very high winds. No one was staying in the hotel that night. The winds were so high that I was moving around the hotel to make sure we hadn't inadvertently left any windows or a door open. I went into room twenty-nine and checked to make sure the windows were secure in there. I walked out of the room and the door just started slamming. I thought it must be the wind. So I went back and double-checked the windows again. I closed the door on the way out of the room, got about halfway down the hall, and it slammed twice again. It was incredible."

VISITING THE SITE

The Island Hotel is a restful interlude from the ordinary. If you plan to attend the Cedar Key Seafood and Craft Festival in mid-October, make reservations well in advance, as the hotels are always fully booked for this event. For shoppers, the boutiques and waterfront shops offer unusual items, many by local artists who have found this island to be one of the few remaining places in Florida where the environment still encourages contemplation. While walking around the island, one can spot rare species of shorebirds. Osprey nests, nestled atop telephone poles, are common. If you weary of the laid-back opulence of the Island Hotel, drive back on S.R. 24 toward the channel bridges. On the left, just before the Back Bayou Bridge (and before the only gas station in Cedar Key) is a small cafe frequented by the locals. "Annie's" is an open-air spot on the sand flats, where, among other seafood dishes, an unforgettable oyster sandwich is served.

DIRECTIONS

From U.S. 19 take S.R. 24 West to Cedar Key, and turn left on 2nd Street, just before the water. The Island Hotel is on the left in the third block. The new owners, Dawn and Tony Cousins, may be reached at (352) 543-5111 for reservations.

REGION TWO

NORTHEAST

FORT CLINCH STATE PARK ON AMELIA ISLAND

One *of the state's most popular* historical sites, Fort Clinch State Park, lies at the tip of Amelia Island, Florida's northernmost barrier island on the eastern coast. Only Cumberland Sound separates it from the state of Georgia. The park covers over eleven hundred acres. Its boundaries include eighty-four hundred feet of shoreline along the sound to the north, and four thousand feet to the east along the Atlantic Ocean. The western boundary is an extensive estuarine marsh system.

Sixty-two campsites are located in the shady hammock and near the beach. The Amelia River, Cumberland Sound, and the Atlantic all provide easy fishing for speckled trout, striped bass, redfish, flounder, and pompano. The three-mile drive from A1A to the fort takes fifteen to twenty minutes, unless the visitor stops to photograph some of the wildlife along the winding road. Overhanging magnolias and other trees shade the drive, and Willow Pond Walk and a nature trail, which are accessible from the road, wind through a hammock and around the pond, where visitors can view wading birds, alligators, and small wildlife. The visitor's center is visible from the ample parking area at the end of the winding entrance road.

The fort was named for General Duncan Lamont Clinch, who was an important figure in the Second Seminole War of the 1830s. Construction on the fort was begun in 1847 by the federal government. Its purpose was to guard the mouth of the St. Marks River, protect coastal and interior shipping, and defend the port of Fernandina, Florida. By 1860, only two bastions, those facing the St. Marys River, had been completed, and the only two walls erected were the walls connecting these two bastions. The ramparts had been installed, and the guardhouse and prison had been completed. Other buildings, such as the lumber sheds, storehouse, and kitchens, were in various stages of completion. Although not a single gun was in position at the outbreak of the war between the North and South, the Confederacy

Fort Clinch

used the fort to protect against attack by sea. Batteries were established in the fort, around the town, and on Amelia and Cumberland Islands. Sand dunes protected some of these installations. Infantry and cavalry also furnished security for this coastal region.

By the year 1862, several South Carolina and Georgia coastal islands had been captured by the North, which left Amelia and Cumberland Islands isolated, causing General Lee to order withdrawal. On March 3rd, the evacuation was completed just as federal gunboats arrived on the shore. Thus the North gained control of Fort Clinch. The 1st New York Volunteer Engineers were brought in at that time to complete construction. In 1867, however, work on the fort was halted, partly because masonry fortification had become obsolete with the development of the rifle cannon, which could throw heavier shot with higher velocity. The Ordnance Department of the Army supervised the fort from 1868 until 1884. In September of 1898, Fort Clinch was declared to no longer be of military value, and all troops were removed. The Engineering Department of the Army kept the fort on caretaker status until 1926, when it was activated again for the Spanish-American War. At that time, according to reports, the drawbridge was rotting and sand blocked the entrance. It lacked drinking water and sanitation facilities.

Fort Clinch was offered for sale in 1926, purchased by private interest, and then sold to the state of Florida in 1935. The Civilian Conservation Corps began development of the park in 1936, and it became one of the first in the Florida Park system, opening to the public in 1938. Fort Clinch was used by the U.S. Armed Forces one last time during World War II. The Coast Guard, jointly with the Army and Navy, maintained a surveillance and communications system in the fort and on local islands to keep watch for landings by spies and saboteurs.

For so old a fort, it is in a remarkable state of preservation. On the first weekend of every month, up to forty volunteers join the rangers to interpret garrison activities for visitors. Demonstrations of fireplace cooking, artillery, marching drills, sentry and infirmary duties take place, and the blacksmith shop, the jail, and other buildings of the fort are all operated much as they were over a century ago. A candlelight viewing is held the first Saturday of each month, the time varying with the hour of sundown.

HAUNT HISTORY

Although soldiers from both sides were stationed at Fort Clinch during the War between the States, neither side used the fort's guns in battle. However, this did not preclude them from experiencing the isolation of battle which manifested as sickness, loneliness, and boredom. Parts of this aged fort have seen soldiers of different wars, in various uniforms, crossing the grounds. We only have written reports to tell the history. The walls could tell many more stories of loss, loneliness, pride, fear, bravery, and loyalty to a cause. These are the stories we will never know.

Park Ranger George Berninger has experienced evidence that some soldiers have refused to leave the fort. Berninger related that during one of the weekend garrison interpretations in which he participates, along with several volunteers, a fellow was asleep in a bunk one night. "He was awakened by the approaching 'clomp-clomp-

clomp' of boots. The sound stopped at his bedside. He was sure someone had come to waken him. He rolled over—and nobody was there." He continued: "One of our women volunteers who lived in the hospital says she has seen a figure dressed all in white, like a nurse, carrying a lantern." Still another "happening" at one of the weekend encampments occurred "during a full moon in July, late at night. Two volunteers were sitting on the porch of one of the barracks when four ghosts in Civil War garb emerged from the northwest bastion tunnel, crossed the parade grounds, marched up the ramp, and disappeared over the wall. The next year, the volunteers made sure they were there again during the July full moon. Sure enough, three ghosts came down the northwest bastion tunnel, marched across the parade ground, and started up the ramp. One volunteer called to them: 'There were four of you last year. Where's the fourth man?' 'He's sick tonight. Couldn't come,' one of the figures called back."

In April 1996, Tim Matthews, a guard who rotates duty with Berninger, relayed the following information while seated in the guardhouse. "One of our volunteers was staying in the top floor of the storehouse at one of our garrisons. She was looking for something in her bags. It was dark and she couldn't see. This other lady walked by carrying a lantern. The volunteer asked if the lady could hold the lantern while she found what she was looking for. So the lady stopped. The volunteer found what she was looking for, and the other lady turned and walked out of the room. The volunteer wanted to thank her. She walked up to the lady and said, 'I appreciate you holding the lantern for me.' The woman looked at her as if to say, 'What are you talking about?' She thought she was being facetious, you know. She said, 'Weren't you just in there holding the lantern for me?' Then she realized it was the wrong woman. And the woman who held the lantern was nowhere to be found."

Over the years many visitors and volunteers have reported hearing the wail of a child in the southwest bastion tunnel. Matthews offered this explanation: "In the twenties or early thirties there was a homeless family living in the fort and they had a baby that died while they were living in there. And what you hear are a baby's cries from the southwest tunnel."

Southwest Tunnel

VISITING THE SITE

Garrisons are held the first weekend of each month, Saturday 9:00 A.M.–5:00 P.M. and Sunday 9:00 A.M.–noon. The park and fort are open every day 9:00 A.M.–5:00 P.M. On Saturday evenings from May through Labor Day, one soldier leads a candlelight tour. Reservations are required for this popular tour. Also during the year are guided nature walks, Easter Sunrise services, a Thanksgiving Holiday Encampment, and a Christmas Encampment. Programs are issued a year in advance, and may be obtained by calling the park. The park entrance fee is $3.25 per car, and an additional $1.00 per person is required for entrance into the fort. Call (904) 277-7274 for reservations and information.

DIRECTIONS

This park is in Fernandina Beach, just off AIA. Signs indicate the entrance to the park.

TABBY HOUSE ON FORT GEORGE ISLAND

A *bit of old Florida* awaits the visitor just off A1A east of the Jacksonville area. Fort George Island, on which the Tabby House is located, is one of a group of islands in the Talbot Islands complex. Ownership of the island is shared by the National Park Service, the state of Florida, and private residents. The section on which the Haunted Tabby House and the Kingsley Plantation (see next chapter) lie has been designated a national park. It is truly a quiet respite for the haunt hunter who also enjoys photography and wildlife. As you enter the narrow road to the park, the haunted Tabby House is in full view on an overhang to the left of the road. Trees in the woods behind the house beckon with their waving arms, taunting the visitor to discover the forest's secrets.

The Tabby House is named after its method of construction. Tabby is a mixture of lime (made by burning oyster shells), sand, and water. This cement was mixed with whole shells and poured into forms. As each layer hardened, the form was moved higher and another layer poured.

HAUNT HISTORY

Construction on the house was originally started by one of the nearby planters, who intended it to be a home for his married daughter. But before the house was finished, he died a violent and unexpected death. The walls now stand with holes where windows and doors were planned, and the shell of the house is occupied only by a ghost.

Many locals can tell you about the house, and several have seen the ghost. The following account appeared in *Scribner's Magazine* in 1877: "Bless yer heart, honey, 'taint allus de same; dat's 'ccordin' to yer sins. Sometimes it's a woman all in white, a-standin' upon de front platform, an' a-wavin' her arms at you; but if yer heart is drefful black an' yer sins awful heavy, why, den it's a great wolf wid eyes like fire."

Tabby House

VISITING THE SITE

Whether or not you have spotted the spirit of Tabby House, continue on the winding shaded drive to the Kingsley Plantation, keeping your eye open for a group of peahens or a family of raccoons trotting down the path. You will pass slave quarters made of tabby, standing in continuous rows. The setting takes you back in time, and on the plantation grounds you can almost hear the big bell calling the slaves from the fields. Even during the summer, you will be treated to a cooling oasis, the constant seabreeze inviting you to stay awhile, relax under the huge trees, and forget the hurried other-life.

As you leave Kingsley Plantation, turn left and follow the Fort George East road to the old golf course shop to pick up a loop guide. There are thirty archaeological sites in the state-owned section of Fort George Island, identified by milepost markers in the guide. Fort George Island has been occupied by humans continuously for five thousand years, and traces of each period remain on the island.

On the southern end of the island lies the Rollins Bird and Wildlife Sanctuary, part of Kingsley Plantation. There are no designated trails here, but the hardy wildlife enthusiast is welcome to explore and photograph the area.

Kingsley Plantation has it all—history, wildlife, nostalgia, beauty, and a serene view of blue water. No food is available in the park, but just south of the entrance is a cafe and grill with a surprisingly large menu and a clean and pleasant atmosphere. Stop here or at one of the small fish camps that dot the highway, so you won't feel rushed while visiting the park. Plan to spend a full day to truly enjoy this piece of Florida. Kingsley Plantation National Park is open from 9:00 A.M. to 5:00 P.M. except Christmas Day, and Tabby House is accessible at all hours. For park information, phone (904) 251-3537.

DIRECTIONS

From I-95 take Hepkscher Exit east. Turn left at the National Park Service sign onto Fort George Island. Follow the signs for Kingsley Plantation. The entrance is one mile east of the Mayport Ferry landing on A1A. The Tabby House is located on the drive to Kingsley Plantation. From the Jacksonville beaches to the south, take the Mayport Ferry across the St. Johns River to A1A. For a ferry schedule, call (904) 246-2922.

Plan to arrive by 1:30 P.M., when a National Park ranger offers a tour of the Kingsley Plantation kitchen and manor house, and narrates a bit of history about the owner, who married one of his slaves.

KINGSLEY PLANTATION

On *the grounds of the Kingsley Plantation* sits the oldest existing plantation house in Florida, believed to date from 1798. Facing the Fort George River, the plantation occupies what is truly one of the most beautiful sites in Florida. It is located on Fort George Island, originally called Alimacani by Native Americans, then San Juan by the Spanish, and finally Fort George by the English. The

Mysterious Apparition at Kingsley Plantation

plantation on this "island by the sea" grew rice, indigo, and later cotton. It is now managed by the National Park Service as part of the Timucuan Ecological and Historic Preserve.

The plantation is best known for being the home of Zephaniah Kingsley , a prominent slave trader, shipbuilder, and planter. Kingsley arrived in the area in 1803 with his African wife Anna Madgigaine Jai Kingsley, a Senegalese slave whom he had freed and married. They moved to Fort George Island in 1813 with their three children. Another was born at Kingsley Plantation. Kingsley also owned property in a large section of northeastern Florida worked by three hundred slaves. Anna managed homesteads, bought and sold slaves, and entered into business agreements with both black and white townspeople. Kingsley's planting operations were very successful, which was probably due to several factors, including management by highly skilled slaves, Kingsley's moderate view of race relations, and the task system used on his plantations.

In 1837, trouble was brewing in this new U.S. territory. The legislature believed free blacks were causing trouble within the slave population. Although history has now proven that, for the most part, free blacks did not act to overthrow slavery, and many were, in fact, slave owners themselves, tensions were high. Harsh punishment and discriminatory laws were passed, causing Zephaniah Kingsley to establish a colony in Haiti for his black wife and their children, along with fifty former slaves whom he had freed and to whom he was paying wages.

Kingsley's family took over operation of the plantation after Kingsley's death, and in 1868, John F. Rollins bought the island. For fifty-five years the Rollins family owned it. It was then deeded to the Fort George Club, which sold it to the state of Florida in 1955.

HAUNT HISTORY

When I first viewed Kingsley Plantation , it was a side trip. The main purpose for my visit to Fort George Island was to photograph and experience the ghost of the Tabby House (see previous chapter). The Kingsley Plantation lies farther down the same road that leads to the Tabby House. Two separate incidents provoked my interest in Kingsley Plantation. The first was a conversation with Kathy, a ranger there, who asked what had brought me to the island and told me that I should definitely talk to Frances Duncan, who used to work there. The second incident was what I saw after some of my slides were developed. As a novice photographer, I am unable to change or modify pictures that I take. There were no other people in my viewing area when I took the photograph reproduced here, yet an image of a woman in white appears on the porch of the plantation house, near the warming kitchen. After interviewing Frances Duncan, I believe I know whose presence is captured in my picture of the Kingsley home.

Frances Duncan, when she was tour guide for the plantation house, lived on the grounds in another structure which has been used for offices and ranger quarters since it was built in the 1920s. "When I worked there, Kingsley House had only two doors that opened to the outside," she told me. "All the rest of the doors were kept locked. I walked into the house one day, and I got an eerie feeling about it. And so I just pulled the door to and walked away. It was just little things like that that happened. Most of the time I was by myself in the house, except when visitors came in for a tour. My daughter said it was poltergeists but that they wouldn't bother me. One time the ranger on duty came over to the house where I lived. It was my day off. He asked me if I had been in the Kingsley house. He said 'Ms. Duncan, when I tried to go into the warming kitchen, the chair that normally sits in the bay window across the room was propped up against the door.' That was the only way you could go into the warming kitchen. I was really upset over that. Another time he told me that he woke up one night and a black man with raggedy cut-off pants, a rope around his waist, and a turban on his head was standing in the corner of his bedroom. He said he tried to wake his wife, but Bonnie was so sound asleep he couldn't wake her up without making a lot of motion and noise. When she did finally rise up, whoever was standing in the corner had disappeared. This happened to him again about three weeks later—the same apparition. It upset Mike real bad, so he decided that he was going to transfer as soon as he could."

She went on: "The warming kitchen is the first room that opens off the porch. That's the way the tour entered. It was my belief that the kitchen was in the basement directly underneath the warming kitchen. When I'd lead a tour into the warming kitchen, people would remark, 'Who's cooking gingerbread?' You could smell gingerbread real strong in there. When you got out of the warming kitchen, you couldn't smell it.

"In the afternoon, before I left for the day, I'd go through the rooms checking to see if everything was in order for the next day. One day I had been upstairs checking, and as I started down, I said, 'Goodnight, Mr. Kingsley.' Then I felt as if someone had poured a bucket of ice water on me. I had goose pimples all over, and so I got out of there. I told a ranger, Gene, about it. He was a good man—a deacon in the church, and I knew he would not make up anything. About a month later, Gene said, 'You told me not to say goodnight to Mr. Kingsley, but I did.' I asked, 'What happened?' He said, 'Somebody poured ice water on me.' So I never did say 'Goodnight Mr. Kingsley' anymore. These things happened over a ten-year span.

"One bed upstairs in Mr. Kingsley's bedroom was placed about two feet from the wall. And at the end of the bed was a window. You couldn't sit on the bed on that side without moving the bed out. One morning I went in, and the bed was pulled out farther. Well, I pushed it back, and the next morning when I went in there the bed was pulled out again. This was right after I had started working there. I pushed the bed back, and when I did, I noticed there were grooves in the wood floor where that bed had been pushed back about fifteen inches. So I called the superintendent of the park, and said 'I want you to see something.' So he came upstairs and looked at it and said, 'Well, what do you think it is?' I said 'I don't know, but every morning when I come in here that bed is pulled out, and there are grooves in this floor where this has been going on for quite a while.' He said, 'Well, it looks like it.' He didn't know what to do about it, so one morning I went in there, and I said, 'OK, you want the bed in the middle of the floor, *leave* the bed in the middle of the floor,' and I turned around and walked out. That bed never moved again. It stayed right where it was.

"I had a spiritualist come in one day, and she was telling me to give her something that was close to me, that I'd handled a lot, and that she could tell me a lot of things about the place. So I took off my key chain and handed it to her. She and I were in the house by ourselves. I wouldn't take her on a regular tour, because I didn't want the other people to hear all that. So she began to tell me about the house: whose room was where, who stayed there, and who lived there. Mr. Kingsley's two sisters lived there. When you go down the latticed-in walkway from Anna Jai's house to the porch at the back of the main plantation house, there is a little room to the left where one of his sisters lived. Another sister lived in the corner room where all the bay windows are on the other side of the house, according to the spiritualist. This sister was the grandmother of James McNeill Whistler, the artist. There used to be a copy of a Whistler painting—Whistler's mother sitting in a chair with her foot on a little stool—in the living room parlor, but they may have taken it out. That spiritualist told me things that were not common knowledge. I had researched it and I knew about it, but it wasn't common knowledge.

"She also told me where the cemetery was. Did you ever know Carita Corse? Carita was a frequent visitor to Kingsley when the Rollins family lived there. I asked her to come out one day and show me where the cemetery was. Standing on the back porch, next to the small bedroom, she said there was a date nut tree right on the edge of it. The date nut palm was still there. And she said it had lots of narcissus that came up every year. Well, there *was* a patch of narcissus that came up every year. The state sent a man down to research the whole area. He said if you would mow this whole area and then leave it for maybe a month, where the graves are will be dark green, and someone can go up in a helicopter and see where the graves are. Well, the state wouldn't do that, so they never did actually find the cemetery, but I believe it was between the house where I lived and Anna Jai's house. That cemetery was in there. I never told this on the tour. The only things I told on the tour were documented facts. I researched the Kingsley family ten years, and have copies of all the wills and documents. Kingsley married an African princess. Of course, he married her according to African ritual. She lived in the little house, and Mr. Kingsley built the other house. They could not live in the same house because they were not considered married here in America."

The strange things that have happened to Ms. Duncan and others at the Kingsley house could have been caused by any number of past residents who, for various reasons, either do not want to or cannot leave the old place. It is highly likely, however, that the ghost of Anna Jai Kingsley returned to Kingsley plantation where she spent many happy years with Zephaniah and their children before having to leave the plantation. Many others have reason to stay there, but the figure of the woman who chose to make herself known in my photograph is most likely Anna.

VISITING THE SITE

Kingsley Plantation is open every day from 9:00 A.M. to 5:00 P.M. except Christmas Day. Guided tours are offered at 9:30 A.M., 11:00 A.M., 1:30 P.M., and 3:00 P.M. Entrance is free. Phone (904) 251-3537 for more information.

DIRECTIONS

Kingsley Plantation is on Fort George Island, north of the Mayport Ferry landing on Rt. A1A. Turn in at the sign and follow the road three miles to the plantation.

CASTILLO DE SAN MARCOS IN ST. AUGUSTINE

The *Castillo de San Marcos*, in St. Augustine, is the oldest masonry fort in the continental United States. Begun in 1672, it took twenty-three years to complete and cost the Spanish Crown over 138,000 pesos, the greatest portion of which went for native labor to obtain shellstone from quarries on Anastasia Island. This rock was called coquina—"tiny shell"—by the Spanish because of all the small shells it contained. The construction brought many workers and their families to settle in the area, stimulating the economy in that region for years. The decision to build this fort was made as a result of pressure from English strongholds in Carolina and a raid on St. Augustine in 1668 by an English pirate. One of the best military engineers, Ignazio Daza, was hired to draw up blueprints and supervise construction. This imposing monument was tested in two critical sieges, proving itself impregnable; it simply absorbed cannonballs fired from enemy ships. One Englishman said that the rock would not splinter, and that the cannonball entered as easily as a knife cutting cheese.

The only blight in this fort's magnificent history is the imprisonment of Osceola, the Seminole leader, and some of his followers. The Seminoles had arrived under a white flag of truce and were captured and imprisoned in Castillo de San Marcos. General Jesup, the officer responsible for this breach of military justice, never lived down the stigma attached to his dishonorable deed.

On July 10, 1821, marking the end of the second period of Spanish control of the Floridas, the Spanish flag was lowered, and the Stars and Stripes was raised over the fort. It was declared a national monument in 1924, and in 1933 the Castillo, including twenty-five acres surrounding the fort, became part of the national park system.

HAUNT HISTORY

Spanish Colonel Garcia Marti and his young wife Dolores arrived in

St. Augustine in July of 1784, shortly after England had ceded the Floridas back to Spain. The fort was an isolated military post, and the heat of summer and mosquitoes would have discouraged any soldier, but Marti was eager to settle in to his new assignment. He had heard great things about Castillo de San Marcos, the massive fortress which had defended St. Augustine since the late 1600s. He showed his wife the fort, taking her through the labyrinths and underground rooms. While walking around the grounds one evening, they met Captain Manuel Abela, the colonel's assistant. Colonel Marti introduced the young officer to his wife. Then he went off to finish reports, and Captain Abela offered to show Dolores the view of the sea from the turrets. Thus began a clandestine romance. They met many times, out under the orange trees by the river, while Colonel Marti was busy familiarizing himself with his new duties. One day he summoned the captain to look over some maps spread out on his desk. When the captain leaned over, Marti smelled the distinctive perfume his wife always wore. He confronted Captain Abela.

Over the next several days the captain failed to answer muster, and finally Marti announced that the officer had been sent to Cuba. Then neighbors inquired about Dolores, after not seeing her for several days. Marti said she had become ill and he had sent her to Mexico to stay with an aunt until arrangements could be made for her to return to Spain.

On July 21, 1833, U.S. engineer Lieutenant Stephen Tuttle was exploring the dungeons beneath Castillo de San Marcos. He found a section of wall which, when tapped, sounded hollow. He chipped away the mortar, and the lantern he held illuminated two skeletons. The soldier later told of the perfumelike smell that filled the passageway when he removed the blocks. Now people who visit the fortress see a strange glow in the darkness at the spot, and a sweet fragrance floats on the dank air of the dungeon.

Joe Mills, a ranger at the fort, told us that Sergeant Brown, who was with the War Department from 1900 to 1925 as caretaker of Fort Clinch, believed that the bones found in the dungeon were those of Captain Abela and Dolores.

The sense of history is so strong at this fort that one can almost feel the ghosts of the men and women who helped develop this outpost, for all of these years a sentinel of Florida.

VISITING THE SITE

The Castillo de San Marcos is open from 8:45 A.M. to 4:45 P.M. every day except Christmas Day. Admission is $2, and children under 16 are admitted free when accompanied by an adult. NPS Golden Age Pass owners are admitted free. Phone (904) 829-3099. The city of St. Augustine can be seen from a horse-drawn carriage, a sightseeing train, or a scenic cruise. The narrow streets invite browsing in the shops that line the brick walkways. The St. Augustine Museum is one of the most complete and interesting museums in the state.

DIRECTIONS

The fort is easy to find at the north end of Avenida Menendez where it meets Castillo Drive. Parking is metered and ample.

ST. FRANCIS INN IN ST. AUGUSTINE

The St. Francis Inn lies in the heart of the historic district of St. Augustine. The entrance is typically Spanish, opening off St. George Street into an enclosed courtyard. The courtyard is reminiscent of a grotto, as banana and palm fronds, a quiet pool, and a weathered statue of St. Francis greet the visitor. The entrance to the main guest house opens off the courtyard.

The inn's history parallels that of St. Augustine, having been occupied by owners who reflect the changing cultural influences on this old city. Over two hundred years ago, in 1791, Gaspar Garcia acquired the land through a Spanish grant. On it he constructed his house of the coquina rock found on nearby Anastasia Island. The house passed through the hands of six additional owners until 1838, when it was purchased by Thomas Henry Dummett. This former

British Marine Colonel was a native of Barbados. Following a slave uprising in Barbados, Dummett moved his family and slaves to Tomoka, Florida, where he bought two plantations. At the outbreak of the Second Seminole War in 1835, Colonel Dummett hurriedly buried the family silver and fled with his family to St. Augustine. There he purchased the old house on St. Francis Street.

Dummet's family lived in the house after his death in 1839, and his widow gave it to their daughters, Anna and Sarah. The house was operated as a boardinghouse and became known as the Dummett House. After Sarah's husband, Major Hardee, acquired ownership of the house, it was known as the Dummett-Hardee House. Major William Hardee was Commandant of Cadets at West Point and published a book that was used as a military textbook for students for many years.

There are indications that Confederate spies operated out of the house during the War between the States. Nothing further is recorded about the house until 1888, when a new owner enlarged the building by adding a third story. During this remodeling, a workman was setting fireplace tiles when he found a bag of doubloons. In his excitement, he left hastily, dropping a few on the way. The worker was never heard from again. In 1925 the old house was bought by the Grahams, who installed bathrooms in each room and a central heating system. Subsequent owners have operated the house as a guest house, and in 1948 the name was changed to the St. Francis Inn.

HAUNT HISTORY

Beverly Lonergan, the manager of St. Francis Inn, discussed the long history of "presences" in the old house. Seated in the comfortable parlor, she recounted several stories of strange happenings experienced by both guests and employees.

"Frequently there are very odd phenomena such as whispering sounds. Up on the third floor is our lowest price room, 3-A. I never say anything to people who stay in that room. Some people have reactions; some people don't. The TV goes on sometimes during the night, and lights go on and off. Some say they hear moans, others whispers. If a lady leaves her pocketbook on a chair, she finds it on the floor."

St. Francis Inn

Beverly continued: "There was a love affair between a soldier and a slave girl. The soldier killed himself on the third floor. One man came and stayed for a week. One day he came running down the stairs: 'Beverly, what is going on in that room up there?' He said things kept turning off and on. He said there was too much going on in that room. 'Just get me out of there!'

"I hear the same from other people. One time I went up to the second floor to find one of the girls who was cleaning. Her name was Connie. I went up there and called her. I *know* she passed me and went into one of the rooms. I followed her into the room and called again. It was very silent. The hairs on my arms stood right up. There was no Connie there. I went back into the hallway and heard the vacuum going. I called again. Connie called back from the third floor. I asked her how she got up there, as I'd just seen her on the second floor. Whoever this person was who went into that room—it wasn't Connie. I don't know if it was a man or woman now. The person had short black hair, and was *carrying towels*.

"I've heard a man's whisper, even down here on the first floor. I can't tell you what he says, but it's a man's whisper. I had an experience in what we call the haunted room, down below. We have a big king bed in there, and we can split it into two beds. One day I was helping one of the girls separate the beds, because they're heavy. There wasn't a soul in the inn—everyone had checked out. I heard the whisper. I asked the girl if she did, and she said, 'I sure did,' and ran out of the room. I ran out after her, telling her not to be scared. It was the man's whisper. It almost sounds like a 'Hello,' but I can't tell for sure.

"Another lady from Daytona came here. She walked around the inn, came down the stairs, and said she was sensitive to spirits. She said, 'You're definitely haunted here. If you talk back to the spirits, they'll usually stop what they're doing. You're haunted, and it's room 3-A.' She said they were good spirits, and that there was more than one.

"A model who stayed here had a big case of makeup, almost like a man's tool chest. She went out to lunch, and there was a horrible rain storm. She came back, went upstairs, and came down furious. She said someone had opened her makeup case that was sitting by the window. It had rained in all around it, and the lid was opened. The strange thing was that, even though the case was sitting at an angle, opened so that the makeup would get wet, nothing was wet in the case—only around it. While she was talking to me, she felt a touch on her neck. She yelled, and said that something was pinching her as she was talking. This was right here in the lobby. She said, 'I feel like someone, or something, doesn't like me.'

"One of our other customers woke up underneath the bed, but couldn't remember how he got there. I've been here seven years, but it is just within the past few years that I've felt this presence. It is usually when I'm fixing coffee or messing with the beds."

A former visitor to the inn, Anita Geordam, has seen a figure she says is "a young black girl, perhaps the slave, who is dressed in white." Ms. Geordam describes her as pleasant and believes she is named Lilly. She said she knew nothing about the inn before staying there. In the evening, before going to bed, she saw what seemed to be a black-and-white figure pass by the dresser, but thought that her eyes were playing tricks on her. Since that time, she and a friend have spent the night in that same room, and she now thinks it is more than her vision. She woke at two o'clock in the morning to find the lamp lit. Her friend denied having turned it on, and when they became aware neither had touched the lamp, they left it alone. After about twenty minutes, the light just as unexpectedly went off. Early the next morning, both of them awoke to a loud noise. They found a purse upside down with the contents spilled out, and the previously locked door was open. The friend also heard the sound of moaning, very distinctly. Ms. Geordam had a shower experience that was very strange. While showering, the water became hotter and hotter, and she finally turned it off, but it turned itself on again. She then told Lilly she had had enough, and to stop this playing around. It worked. On another visit, Ms. Geordam was staying again in 3-A, but noted that nothing unusual had happened that evening. However, the woman in the room below 3-A reported feeling "energy" in her room and heard moaning, which her husband did not hear. She felt it was a friendly presence, though, and was not frightened.

Marie Register, who together with her husband worked at the inn for eight years, said that guests in 3-A repeatedly saw and heard strange things, particularly "flowing figures." One guest specifically requested room 3-A so that he could use his Ouija board, because that seemed to be the only place it would work for him. He also told her, without knowing her name, that someone by the name of Register was going to work at the inn for the next four years. She denied that she would be staying there four more years, but that is exactly how long she stayed.

A later innkeeper, Jeanette Boerema, is reported to have said "something happens every time; a book will fall over or a picture will move." She has also heard the strange moaning sound and has seen a figure. One night she walked up the steps before going to bed for the evening and saw a lady with a slight build and long dark hair going down the back staircase. She later realized there was no one staying at the inn who could have been that figure, and when she realized that, the figure disappeared. Another time, Mrs. Boerema was in 3-A with her college-age children when the lamp went on. Soon all three heard a mournful wail. They quickly left the room and closed the door, but they could still hear the wail.

Susan Mills spent the night in 3-A. In the early morning hours, she woke to a loud "thump," and discovered that a bag she had placed carefully in a chair was dumped upside down on the floor. She insisted the "thump" was far too loud to be the tote bag and its contents, which were nothing but news clippings and papers—her notes on the history of the St. Francis Inn.

VISITING THE SITE

Guest accommodations in this historic old house are modestly priced, with varying accommodations. A continental breakfast is served each morning in the inn. Patrons may use the bicycles kept at the inn to tour St. Augustine and visit the quaint shops and sites along the bayfront. Reservations or information may be obtained by writing the inn at 279 St. George Street, St. Augustine, FL 32084, or by calling (904) 824-6068 or (800) 824-6062.

Very near the St. Francis Inn is the St. Augustine Historical Society Library. History buffs should allow ample time to browse, as this library houses records of the oldest city in a comfortable and friendly atmosphere which will delight anyone interested in Florida's very early years.

DIRECTIONS

At the southern end of Avenida Menendez is St. Francis Street. Maps and layouts of St. Augustine are easily found, with historical homes prominently located. Just looking for this home makes for an enjoyable stroll.

46 AVENIDA MENENDEZ IN ST. AUGUSTINE

T*he development of St. Augustine*, taking place over a period of five centuries, has been documented by records both in the U.S. and in Europe. It is the oldest permanent European settlement in the United States. The oldest house in St. Augustine still standing was built between 1702 and 1727. It was during the so-called First Spanish period, which lasted until 1763, that the building at 46 Avenida Menendez, which now houses a restaurant, was built, originally of tabby. The first owner was Juana Navarro, who was born in 1729 in St. Augustine. She also owned another home on St. George Street, now known as the Ribera House. Juana married Salvador Francisco de Porras, and together they had at least nine children. One, named Catalina, was born in 1753. Ten years later, the Treaty of Paris was signed, and Florida became a British colony after nearly two hundred years of Spanish rule. The entire population of St. Augustine evacuated to Cuba, the de Porras family among them.

British soldiers moved into the vacated homes, and many Loyalists from the north and from England also came here to begin a new life. The de Porras house was claimed by Walton & Company of New York. Later, around 1784, East Florida returned to Spanish rule. The Loyalists became disenchanted, and with the outgoing British, moved away to avoid having to swear allegiance to the Spanish crown and converting to Catholicism. During these years, Catalina de Porras had grown and married Joseph Xavier Ponce de Leon. Salvador de Porras had died, and his widow, Catalina's mother Juana, with the help of her son-in-law Ponce de Leon, returned from Cuba to claim her property.

Since the homes had been neglected, many were in such disrepair that the governor planned to auction them. However, the de Porras house was never auctioned, thanks to the intervention and persistence of the de Porras family, and they eventually gained back their rightful home. Later the de Porras heirs sold the home to Joseph Lorrente, who worked tirelessly repairing the home until his sudden death in 1813 on a ship at sea during a hurricane. His widow then sold the home to Charles W. Bulow, who was a wealthy plantation owner in South Carolina and in Florida. His son John Joachim later inherited the bayfront home as well as the entire Bulow Bay Plantation, which was burned during the Second Seminole War. Only the sugar mill ruins remain on what is now a state historic site near Flagler Beach.

When Florida became a United States territory, Bulow's heirs sold the home to Margaret Cook, who later sold it to Buroughs E. Carr. Carr opened a general store next to the home. A few years later, a fire raced through the bayfront and plaza areas of St. Augustine, destroying many homes, among them the original de Porras place. However, Carr was able to rebuild the home true to its original Spanish structure, based on sketches that had been done in 1840. This time, though, poured concrete instead of tabby was used in the rebuilding.

The next owner was Bartolo Genovar. He was a prominent businessman who opened the first opera house in St. Augustine. Sidney Harrison, the chief clerk for the Florida East Coast Railway Company, purchased the house from Genovar. In 1914 there was another fire, but this time the house was untouched. The next owners were the Maclennens. Mrs. Maclennen was a relative of Henry Flagler, the railroad magnate, and her husband was a railroad contractor. After Mrs. Maclennen's death, the house changed owners several times, finally passing to John Drysdale, who was elected governor in 1827. His descendant, W. B. Drysdale, owner of the St. Augustine Alligator Farm, lived there until 1976, when he sold the house to be used as a restaurant, the Puerta Verde. Later, the home on 46 Avenida Menendez, formerly known as Bay Street, was The Chart House Restaurant, and then, Catalina's Gardens. It was named after Catalina de Porras, whose childhood ties to the home were strong enough to cause her to return from Cuba and relentlessly work to regain her family home. In 1997 the property again changed ownership, and was renamed Harry's Seafood Bar and Grille.

HAUNT HISTORY

During the time the de Porras home was being used as the Chart House Restaurant, two employees witnessed unusual presences. Lynn

Cumiskey remembers the day she was washing uniforms: "They were sitting in a laundry basket on the floor. I walked by and noticed this funky smell, and then I saw smoke coming from the basket— not from the top, but from down inside, underneath the clothes." Upon inspection, some of the uniforms were found to have been burned, although "no one was smoking and no matches were near the basket." She remembered that the house had a history of fire, which made the event even stranger. Another employee, William St. John, remembered seeing movements out of the corner of his eye. "You look and no one is there." He said he was very nervous while he worked there.

Jim Martini, the past owner of what was then called Catalina's Gardens, was interviewed when he owned the property, and admitted that strange things indeed happen there. The female ghost has come to be known as Bridgett. "There was a fire, and she was one of the only people who died during the fire. People have different beliefs about how or why she is seen," he said. "Sometimes you walk into a room and notice a strange kind of scent, an aroma. And at times, when we haven't used a room in a month, there will be things on the carpet. There's no reason to have something like that happen. Things have been moved around in the restaurant. And at times when you're here alone in the evening, you'll hear things. It's an old home, so it has its cracks and crevices and wind patterns, but you get a chill. My partner, Rick Worley, was here as general manager for The Chart House. They were here for a number of years. He has some stories about when he was doing inventories or paperwork and felt a presence. We bought the restaurant from the Chart House in 1993. Psychics came in, and they said there was an obvious presence in the ladies' room upstairs."

Is Bridgett, one of the few victims of the fire, still in residence in the house? Or is Catalina still there, overseeing the home she and her family struggled to regain? Happenings indicate the female presence either doesn't want to leave or can't leave. However, she does not disturb the present owners, who go about their everyday business sometimes accompanied by a silent partner.

VISITING THE SITE

Facing the Mantanzas River and Intracoastal Waterway, 46 Avenida

Menendez is in one of the prettiest locations in St. Augustine and within walking distance of several historic places the visitor will not want to miss. Harry's Seafood Bar and Grille now occupies the old house. The veggie pasta and a glass of wine make a perfect interlude to sightseeing. Happy hour is from 2:00 P.M. to 7:00 P.M. daily, with half-price wings and oysters and reduced bar prices. Lunch is served until 4 P.M., dinner from 4 P.M. until closing. Harry's is open Sunday–Tuesday from 11:00 A.M. to 10:00 P.M., and Wednesday–Saturday from 11:00 A.M. to 11:00 P.M.

DIRECTIONS

From U.S. 1 turn east onto King Street. When approaching the Bridge of Lions, turn left onto Avenida Menendez. Harry's Seafood Bar and Grille is on your left.

LIGHTKEEPER'S HOUSE IN ST. AUGUSTINE

T*he shifting sands at the seaward entrance* to colonial St. Augustine were dreaded by French and Spanish adventurers alike. The shallow inlet was so treacherous the Spanish called it "Crazy Banks." In 1565, at the beginning of the Spanish expansion in *La Florida*, Spanish settlers erected a wooden watchtower at the shallow harbor to guide supply ships and allow sentries to warn of enemy vessels approaching St. Augustine. In 1824 the tower officially became Florida's first lighthouse. Erosion weakened the wooden structure over time, and in 1875 the old lookout was replaced with the current one, farther from the eroding waves. At that time a brick keeper's house was added.

This lighthouse was electrified in 1936; prior to this, keepers heated tallow in fireplaces to furnish the flame, later using kerosene. A system of weights was used to turn the light at the top of the lighthouse so that it would be visible from the water. Keepers had to haul fuel up the 219 steps every night. This was a daunting physical task performed by all the keepers, some of whom were women. An arsonist's fire raged through the keeper's house in 1970, but it has since been restored. The St. Augustine light is still used as an aid to navigation. During World War II, the lights were dimmed so that enemy ships outside the shipping lanes could not detect U.S. submarines which may have been patrolling the shores.

The present Fresnel lens is the original one installed in the tower when it was built. It is a first-order lens, a nine-foot-tall lens used for seacoasts (as opposed to progressively smaller lenses, the smallest of which, sixth-order lenses, are primarily used in harbors). The St. Augustine light may be seen from a distance of nineteen to twenty-five nautical miles before the earth's curvature blocks it from sight.

Cracks are evident in the structure, caused by shock waves from an earlier earthquake. But the real threat to these sentinels is ever-increasing technology, not hurricanes or people (as most believe), so they are frequently being saved by various historic or civil groups, who strive to protect these "guiding lights" for the enjoyment of succeeding generations.

HAUNT HISTORY

According to John Lienlockken, who helped restore the keeper's house after the fire, many bizarre incidents occurred when he was working there. "We were working up on scaffolding inside and putting up pigeon blocks. I turned around and had this image or thought of someone hanging up there. I told my partner about it. It really shook me up." Later, Jake, a man who had a business near the lighthouse and had spoken to the keeper on several occasions, told John that indeed a "visitor from the sea" hanged himself in the building in the 1930s. Jake said he "used to see lights" coming from the house after the fire. Swain, the keeper, said that every time he walked from the house to the tower, footsteps would follow him. The footsteps never came into the house, but only followed him up and back down the tower. John, the construction worker, said so many acci-

St. Augustine Lighthouse

dents happened there that he and his partners, Michael Gourely and Wayne Pierce, quit after six months and got other jobs.

Kathleen Steward, the bright young lady who gives tours of the lighthouse, said, "One day about a month ago, I was driving up the entrance road and I saw that the door was open. I thought that was unusual, but I figured that Jeff, the museum director, must have come in early. It turned out he hadn't. I saw someone tall, leaning over the rail. I drove in and parked, and went over to the lighthouse. The alarm wasn't on; I don't know why. I went up there, and no one was there. I never saw anyone leaving. I looked and listened, and there was no one. Someone could have gotten hold of the key and gone up there—that is the only explanation— and then came down while I was parking the car. It was the figure of a tall man, leaning over the railing. I think it was a ghost."

During the 1850s, Andreau, one of the keepers, fell to his death while painting the first light tower, necessitating that his wife take over the duties of keeper. Does Andreau's ghost haunt the grounds and tower, or is it the ghost of the "man from the sea" who died from hanging?

VISITING THE SITE

An easy walk up the 219 steps takes the visitor to the top of the 165-foot-tall lighthouse tower for a breathtaking view of St. Augustine and the beaches. You can encircle the tower top for a view of the entire area. Even on a sweltering July day in Florida, it's cool at the top of the tower, looking out over the Atlantic. Fees are $4 for adults, $3 for seniors, and $2 for children. Children must be four feet tall and seven years old to climb the tower. Winter hours are 9:30 A.M.–5:00 P.M. daily. Summer hours are 9:30 A.M.–6:30 P.M. Monday through Thursday, and 9:30 A.M.–8:00 P.M. Friday through Sunday. The tower closes one half hour before the museum. Call ahead if the weather is questionable, as it is closed during rain or heavy wind, as well as on Easter, Thanksgiving, and Christmas Day. For information call (904) 829-0745.

Across from the lighthouse is the Lighthouse Park Restaurant, which is open for breakfast, lunch, and dinner. Located on the water, it is the perfect place to end your lighthouse trip. There is a varied menu, but almost everyone orders one of their specialty salads. Phone (904) 826-4002.

DIRECTIONS

Off A1A South, turn east onto Old Beach Road across from the Alligator Farm, and follow the signs.

DEVIL'S MILLHOPPER NEAR GAINESVILLE

A *state park lying within minutes* of the bustling university town of Gainesville, Devil's Millhopper is an oasis for the spirit. The name Millhopper is derived from the sinkhole's rounded sloping shape.

A millhopper is a funnel-like device at the top of a grist mill into which the grain is poured for grinding. Because fossils and bones were found in the bottom of the sinkhole, early settlers believed that this was the millhopper that fed bodies to the devil. So it became the Devil's Millhopper.

This huge sinkhole is 117 feet deep and 500 feet across. Sinkholes are formed as rainwater soaks into the ground, passing through plant material. This action increases the amount of acid in the water, already a weak carbonic acid from previous contact with carbon dioxide in the air. When this water reaches the hard limestone layer, small cavities are formed as the acid water slowly dissolves the rock. Eventually the ceiling of the cavern becomes so thin that it collapses under the weight of the earth above it, falling to the bottom. Slopes of this sinkhole, the state park system's only geological site, provide a history of Florida's past: skeletons of marine animals may be seen in the lower layer, while upper levels display the fossilized remains of now-extinct land animals who roamed this area after the sea level dropped.

Ten different species of oaks are found in this sixty-three-acre park. The park itself includes a sand hill, the hammock, and the swamp. Occasional fires sweep through the area and kill the invading hardwoods, maintaining the wide spacing of the trees which allows enough sunlight to reach the forest floor to let a covering of grasses and flowering plants thrive. The gopher tortoise and many other small mammals, birds, and other wildlife find the twelve springs in the park to their liking.

It is a short drive from the paved road back to the park entrance.

Devil's Millhopper

The parking area is ample, with several shaded spots. Picnic tables sit under tall pines that shade visitors from the Florida sun. The visitors' center has an ongoing, taped message to accompany a film that explains the Native American legend of the site. Clear, well-drawn graphics explain the geological significance of the Devil's Millhopper.

Continuing toward the center of the park on the pine needle path from the visitors' center to the sinkhole, we begin to relax and enjoy this unusual park. A half-mile nature trail follows the rim, and for those who don't want to descend and then climb the stairs, the trail offers different vantage points from which to view the sinkhole from above. Approaching the flight of 232 steps, the coolness surprises us. For a moment, we imagine ourselves in the Smoky Mountains walking down a cool path, and we have to remind ourselves we are in Florida. The numerous waterfalls keep the air cool and moist. The path that circles the sinkhole is high, and as you look over the edge, the incline is steep. Signs warn the visitor of the delicate vegetation at the inner edge of this giant funnel. As we begin to descend the steps, the creeks and waterfalls draw us into another world. The light changes to shadows, and the shadows to light.

Several landings provide chances to photograph this unique place. If you go on a morning in April, as I did, there are few others in the park, and you can hear the tears of the Indian braves splashing on the rocks at every turn of the steps.

HAUNT HISTORY

In November of 1928, the *Gainesville Sun* ran an article on Mammy Clifton, then age ninety-four. She related that her father and brother were on their way home from town with a wagonload of cotton. She was very young at the time. She said Ed, her brother, "were full up wid likker. We kept on a walkin' when all ob a sudden de geround trembelled and shook so hard dat ah almos fell down." They kept on walking, but later decided to wait for Ed, who was following behind them. When he did not appear, they went back for him. "Jes den we come up on de mos' awfullest thing ah ever did see in mah life. Right in de front ob us dey was a monstrous hole. De groun' jes' naterrly wasn'. Pappy, he began ter shoutin' ter God. Ah would hav done de same thing but ah couldn't. Ah was shore scairt . . . putty soon along come daylight. Den we looked down inter dat hole. Trees and bushes was all a-layin' helter skelter on to each other, what wasn' covered up wid water. An' den we see'd him. Dar was Ed, floating on his back in dat water. Dat shore war terrible. . . . Dey waren' no puhson brave 'nough to go down inter dat hole—everybody too scairt ob de debbil."

Park manager Randy Brown said he was told that the devil had fallen in love with a native maiden. She spurned his advances, however, and refused his marriage proposal. One night, the devil kidnapped the maiden. He snatched her in his arms and ran through the pine woods. A posse of braves raced to her rescue. Just as they were about to overtake the devil, the demon whirled and turned the braves into stone. The devil caused this huge hole to open up, and he disappeared into it with the maiden. Now the braves' tears trickle constantly from the stone. When the moon is full, a sensitive ear can hear the occasional scream or moan of a maiden as she calls.

VISITING THE SITE

Because of reduced funding for our parks, this one, like many others, relies on the honor system for parking. Bring correct change for the

$2.00 fee, which is dropped into a chute as you enter. The ranger gives a guided tour and talk only on Saturdays at 10 A.M. Bring a picnic lunch to enjoy the day in this quiet setting.

DIRECTIONS

Devil's Millhopper is located two miles northwest of Gainesville. Take Exit 77 (C.R. 222) off I-75. After about two and a half miles, turn left onto 43rd Street. At the next traffic light, turn left. The park is on the right. Call (904) 462-7905 for information.

HERLONG MANSION IN MICANOPY

Stately old pecan and oak trees drape their moss-covered arms around Herlong Mansion, as if to protect it from modern intrusion. In this seductive shade once stood the modest home of the Herlong family. As the family wealth increased with the expansion of their timber and citrus holdings, the Herlongs built a Classic Revival mansion over the original two-story house. Its interior has been slightly remodeled to accommodate guests who frequent what is now a popular bed-and-breakfast, but the house remains almost as it was when the Herlongs were there. Huge Roman-style columns support a double verandah onto which some of the bedrooms open. The interior is a reminder of elegance with its leaded glass windows, abundant use of mahogany, and maple inlaid floors. Located in Micanopy, one of Florida's oldest towns, it reflects the Southern charm of the quiet village.

During the sixteenth and seventeenth centuries, Timucua tribes lived in this interior region of Florida. It was later the Seminole village of Cuscowilla. Later, Fort Micanopy was built but was burned during the Seminole War. After the war, settlers built homes and farms around what is now Micanopy. Cholokka Boulevard, the town's main street, was once a path used by Native Americans to trade their

Herlong Mansion

wares. From this early history to the present day, the town has retained its rural appeal. Even now, only about eight hundred people live in Micanopy. Just twelve miles south of Gainesville, the town has, remarkably, retained the quiet ambiance of old Florida. The busiest it ever gets is in November when townspeople block off the only main street for the Micanopy Fall Festival. Antique shops and bookstores are the only noticeable businesses in Micanopy.

T*he history of the old house* tells the story of a family. Near the turn of the century, Zetty Clarence Herlong's wife, Natalie, inherited a simple homestead in Micanopy, and they and their six children moved there from South Carolina. After Zetty's successful ventures in Florida, he built the mansion, although the property remained in Natalie's name. When she passed away, the mansion was left to her children equally, with the understanding that their father could live there until his death. He lived another ten years. During this time, the mansion was not kept up, but when their father died, all the children wanted it for their personal residence. However, only one of the siblings, Inez, could afford it. Inez's husband, Fletcher Miller, had died, and she was left with enough money to buy out the other children.

Inez worked on restoring the house, which had fallen into disrepair. She was making a bed in an upstairs bedroom when she had a heart attack and died. She never got to enjoy the house as she planned. Perhaps because the family was broken apart over ownership of the house, or because she just loved the homestead and had spent years of enjoyment in it when she was young, she now wants to stay.

HAUNT HISTORY

"'Ghostbusters' were here," Sonny Howard, owner of Herlong Mansion Bed and Breakfast, told me. "The Center for Paranormal Studies, out of Ocala, works nationwide. These are educated people. Dr. Nichols heads it up, and he has a PhD in Psychology." Called the 'ghostbusters' by their friends, the group that investigated Herlong Mansion consists of Andrew Nichols, a psychologist; Russell McCarty, an anthropologist; and James Bosworth, a biochemist. They have appeared on the television show 'Unsolved Mysteries,' and have a reputation for thorough investigations.

Howard continued: "The *Gainesville Sun* and the *Ocala Star-Banner* had Dr. Nichols come here. He feels that ghosts are electromagnetic energy created by some traumatic experience, and he thinks they are real. He brought an electromagnetic meter and an infrared camera, and when he walked down the hallway on the second floor toward the back of the house, his gauge went all the way off the end and came back. He's been back twice. I invited him to stay the night as my guest, and I put him in the room, but nothing happened."

He explained that "the room" was Inez's sister Mae's room, and was the room in which Inez died. "Sometimes something will happen two or three times a week, and sometimes nothing will happen for a month. And what I don't know is if people aren't telling me everything. The only thing that's happened to me personally is that, sitting here dealing with the telephone, I have heard the door of that room open and close on more than one occasion. It makes a unique sound, so I know which door it is. Then when I go and check, there's nobody here but me. I was scared at first, but after six years, and not having seen a single scary thing happen, my conclusion is that she's happy, and as long as she's happy, I'm happy. She lived through an eighteen-year family fight to get the house; it split the family, and nobody ever spoke to anybody again. She died here the day she took possession, and she never had a chance to enjoy it after fighting for it for eighteen years. Then her son Buddy Miller got it. He was the last family member to own it, and he sold it in eighty-six to the previous owners, the Evanses.

"I've had people come here before I even bought the house and say things have always happened in that one room. One guy rented the whole house, for fifty dollars a month, when it needed a lot of work. He said they locked the two doors to that room, and you could hear those doors rattling all night long. When they unlocked them, everything stopped."

Mr. Howard told me that the former owners had hired a crew that specialized in historic restoration and preservation work. They slept a few nights in the old house, but after hearing doors opening and closing, and footsteps in the night, they refused to sleep in the house or work in there after dark. The owners, anxious to show the workers there was nothing in the house, stayed there themselves one night. They locked the door. In the morning the door had been unlocked and stood ajar. Howard said there was no doubt—Inez was still in her mansion. "There are probably a thousand instances that I have been told about: dreams, two sightings, specific things that have happened, like the door, the lights, the clock radio. Two ladies (unrelated) said they were awakened at different times by refreshing mists of water on their face. A few months ago, a woman going through a divorce said she had the best night's sleep she'd had in six months. It's always that room. I don't know how to explain it. If it had just been one or two things, you could just say it's just an old house, but when there have been a thousand, and it's one room, there's got to be some basis for it."

A letter Howard keeps, from one of his guests, reads: "I want to tell you how much we enjoyed your house and Inez. I may have met Inez, but didn't say anything at breakfast. When we turned in for the night, Nancy was reading and I was trying to sleep. I rolled over and opened my eyes. There in the mirror over the dressing table was an apparition floating across the room. It couldn't be seen in the room itself, only in the mirror. It had a red shawl or hood over its head, and I couldn't make out the facial features, though I felt it was a woman." Mr. Howard will frequently ask his guests at breakfast the next morning how they slept. Sometimes strange things have happened, sometimes not. Ghostbuster Nichols said, "This is a classic haunting. There is definitely something here." Sonny Howard confided, "I could have Nichols come back and get rid of Inez, but why should I? She's not bothering anybody."

VISITING THE SITE

Herlong Mansion Bed and Breakfast is a totally nonsmoking establishment and is always filled on football weekends at the University of Florida. Call (352) 466-3322 well ahead for reservations. If you get tired of browsing in the lovely bookstores and antique shops in Micanopy, Paynes Prairie State Preserve and the Marjorie Kinnan Rawlings home at Cross Creek are both within a short drive of the town.

DIRECTIONS

Traveling south from Gainesville, take the Micanopy exit off I-75. Follow the signs to Micanopy. Herlong Mansion is at 402 NE Cholokka Boulevard.

WASHINGTON OAKS STATE GARDENS NEAR ST. AUGUSTINE

E*xtending from the Atlantic Ocean* to the Matanzas River across A1A, Washington Oaks State Gardens preserves not only habitat for our endangered Florida scrub jay, pileated woodpecker, and gopher tortoise, but also some original coastal scenery. The eastern section of this four-hundred-acre park is open for fishing and swimming, but it is better known for its picturesque beach which has boulders that, at low tide, protect many shore birds as they feast on the ocean's tasty deposits such as starfish and crabs. The coquina rocks are part of a sedimentary formation that underlies most of the Atlantic shore, but is covered by sand except for the small strip of land between Marineland and Washington Oaks' southern boundary. About a hundred thousand years ago, when the sea level was higher than it is now, sand and shells formed offshore bars. Later, the sea level dropped, leaving the bar exposed. Rainwater moving through the layers dissolved calcium carbonate, forming a cement matrix that turned the loose sediment into rock. For many thousands of years these rocks stood above sea level, until melting glaciers, about seven thousand years ago, raised the sea level again. Waves carved the rocks into the formations we see today. There are giant blowholes and unusual layers of red sands between layers. There are tubes that may be marine worm tubes or holes made by roots growing in the sand before it hardened. There are potholes to be seen, some with the smooth stones known as "grind stones."

On the west side of A1A lies a lush hammock of live oaks and magnolias, bordered by the marshes of the Matanzas River. The gardens lie in this hammock area.

Past the entrance gate a beautiful drive leads to the south end of the park. This main road offers access to the gardens, a parking area, and hiking trails. One of these trails, the Malacompra, passes through the maritime hammock bordering the estuarine tidal marsh. You can leave the interpretive center at the entrance to the gardens and follow the trail along the river to the picnic area. This is a shady hammock with a pavilion and grills, restrooms, and a few swings and bars for playing children. A very quiet place, it is ideal for an artist to work. Everywhere you look are subjects for the talented who can translate this beauty into an image for our pleasure.

The interpretive center itself has a big brick patio out back, with welcoming chairs where visitors can relax and watch the river. All is shaded and cool, even in July.

The gardens have many reflecting waterpools, and the azaleas, camellias, and roses are unsurpassed. Many species of exotic plants from around the world are found along footpaths in the formal gardens. There is a hill at the top of the rose garden which contains oyster shells and discards left by Native Americans. Archaeology studies are currently underway to learn more about the lives of the native people who lived here.

In 1815, the land was part of a Spanish land grant to Bautista don Juan Ferreira. It was bought by Jose Mariano Hernandez in 1818, and developed as a plantation which he named "Belle Vista." Although ownership remained in his family for over a hundred years, there is no evidence that anyone connected with the family lived here until the 1870s. In 1821, when Florida became a U.S. territory, Hernandez changed his name to Joseph Marion Hernandez. He was known as General Hernandez, because, as Brigadier General, he organized and commanded militia during the Second Seminole War. In 1836, Native Americans burned plantations along the Matanzas River, including Hernandez's lands.

In 1845, Hernandez's daughter Luisa married a lawyer from North Carolina named George Lawrence Washington, a relative of President George Washington. He built a house at Belle Vista, which later burned. Today huge oaks grow on the site where the house stood, and a Y-shaped path on the site turns toward the river. A plaque on the footpath indicates the site.

Only an economic twist of fate, the end of the Florida land boom, kept the property from being turned into a subdivision when one of Washington's heirs, in 1923, sold the land to developers. It was to be called "Hernandez Estates." In 1936, Louise Clark bought the land for a retirement home for her and her third husband, Owen D. Young. Young was an attorney who had been chairman of the board of General Electric and RCA. They named the place "Washington Oaks." One of their children, Virginia, died here. Mr. Young died in 1962, and Mrs. Young in 1965, shortly after bequeathing Washington Oaks to the state of Florida, specifying that the gardens be "maintained in their present form."

HAUNT HISTORY

Many stories surround this lovely park. Before it became a state park, locals insisted that a light "moved in the vicinity of the house that burned." The light was the size of a train beacon and could not be caught. Once two brothers, determined to reach the source of the light, wrecked their car trying to catch it. The light, it is said, is a lantern carried by Hernandez, looking for his former home. Native Americans did burn his lands; perhaps he wanders the property, wanting to stay near the site he owned.

More recently, reports of missing or moved items abound. Cheryl, one of the rangers tending to the horticultural gardens, told us that, indeed, strange things still happen here. "There was a ranger walking up near the interpretive center, and there wasn't a breeze blowing. He was making his rounds, walking out to check the trash out by the seawall, and the doors started rattling—and they were all closed." Things are frequently missing or moved, with no explanation. Some who have witnessed strange happenings believe Hernandez's spirit remains at Washington Oaks. Others say that Virginia, the daughter of Owen Young, who died there, left her presence to be felt. Certainly both their spirits may linger in this beautiful place in Florida which embraces the Matanzas River.

VISITING THE SITE

Pack a picnic, enjoy the beach area with its unusual boulders on the Atlantic side, and plan to take a leisurely walk through the gardens. This is a photographer's paradise. The entrance fee is $3.25 per vehicle, which includes up to eight people. Watch for gophers crossing the road, even before you reach the gate. Even the parking area by the gardens is shaded with huge trees. When it's too hot in St. Augustine, this is the perfect side trip.

DIRECTIONS

Take A1A south from St. Augustine or north from Daytona. Washington Oaks lies one mile south of Marineland.

REGION THREE

CENTRAL EAST

DAYTONA PLAYHOUSE IN DAYTONA BEACH

The *entrance to the Daytona Playhouse* faces the Halifax River. The ivory building with maroon awnings, surrounded by palms and pink crepe myrtle, makes a lovely sight. Productions have been held in this active theater since 1956, including Broadway shows and musicals using local talent. Inside, the Playhouse is quiet except for the workers on stage, building the set for the opening production of the new season. It appears to be just another small community theater. The anticipation of good entertainment is there, even with the empty seats. But this theater is different. Here there are more than the thespians, more than the audience, when the curtain rises.

HAUNT HISTORY

The set was being prepared for a presentation of *Oklahoma!* when I visited the Daytona Playhouse. Coincidentally, it was at a 1972 performance of *Oklahoma!* that Alice Frey Winchester was supposed to be hoisted to the shoulders of her dancing partner during the finale. He lost his grip, and "almost dropped me in the orchestra pit." Jim Lewis, her partner, explained to her that he had seen a transparent figure of a woman wearing a large plumed hat, and in his surprise was distracted from the routine.

Mr. John S. Barnett, the technical director for the Daytona Playhouse, shared with me notes and a report from his files on the Playhouse investigation in 1982, when a psychic group from Daytona Beach Community College came to the theater to investigate the entities who were so persistent. Contact was made with an attractive young lady with strawberry-blonde hair, wearing a flamingo-peach-colored gown with plumes. She said her name was Alice, and the last name sounded, to several members of the group, like Beckwith. She told them her lover, Andre Dorn (or Doern), had left the white fifteen-room house in which they lived and gone to Spain to fight in the 1930s. She had been expecting their first child. She sank into a deep depression, and one day left the house and walked into the Halifax River.

Many people have described an apparition of a man who walks about the theater. He is seen around the dressing room in the stage area, as well as seated in the audience, watching productions. He is dressed in a dapper 1930s fashion, with a scarf or cape thrown across one shoulder. When the psychics made contact with Alice's spirit, they later saw an older man backstage, described as an unhealthy-looking foreigner, possibly Italian. He seemed to be showing them a gold ring with a round onyx setting in the shape of a bull's head with green eyes. The ring seemed to be connected with their search. At another time, two hands were seen showing them a large blue jewel, which also seemed to carry some significance, although they never found out what.

There are two graves in the Greenwood cemetery in Daytona Beach that bear the name Beckwith. The investigation indicates that Alice and Andre are tied to the property, although not necessarily to the theater itself, as Alice described a fifteen-room house in which she lived. The playhouse was built on the property in 1956. Courthouse records in Volusia County indicate that property was owned by both the Beckwith and Doern families in the vicinity of where the playhouse now stands, as was indicated in the Peters report in the office files at the Playhouse. The two entities are not together, and the group felt that Doern seems confused and on a different "plane of existence" than Alice. This could be because he was killed in Spain and returned to find Alice, not knowing that she had died in the Halifax River.

Alice Winchester and Terry Bacon, a teacher at Spruce Creek High School who has been involved with the Playhouse for several years, were alone in the building one Saturday morning working on painting the set for a performance of *Finian's Rainbow*. Suddenly a man appeared, and one of the women asked if she could help him. He appeared to take no notice of the two women, and continued toward the dressing room, where he pulled aside the privacy curtain and went in. Getting no response from the man, the two workers also entered the room, and no one was there. There was no way to get out except the entrance through which they had come. A small jalousie window

Daytona Playhouse

was the only other opening—too small for anyone to fit through. The volunteer workers described the man as short with a mustache. "He was wearing a bow tie and a red coat with an insignia on the pocket, white pants and a white shirt; very dapper-looking." That was August 1974. And sitings of both Andre and Alice have continued since then.

Frequently things happen without people actually seeing the perpetrator. Kelly Koscoe, a young actress at the Playhouse, said that she was sitting in a chair beside a door which leads from the audience to the stage, waiting for her cue to go onstage. The door beside her opened and slowly closed again. No one was there—only a cool breeze came in beside her.

The ghosts appear harmless, pleasant, searching, and very sad. The psychic group, whose hope it was to lead the entities to the light, to the "other world" where their spirits would be at rest, was unsuccessful. So Alice and Andre continue to be an ongoing part of the plays, of the audience, of the atmosphere of the theater. And the shim-

Set of *Oklahoma!*

mering blue Halifax River, seen from the entrance to the playhouse, continues to hide its secret.

VISITING THE SITE

Unless you are a motorcycle enthusiast, try to visit Daytona Beach sometime other than the first week of March. A ten-day bikers' event is held annually around that time, drawing five hundred thousand people. In February and July there are Speedway events, which also draw thousands, but since they are one-day events, visitors can usually work around those dates. Historic sites and museums abound, and wildlife refuges are abundant along the coastal area. The LPGA maintains its headquarters in Daytona Beach and has just built a new course which is open to the public. The Daytona Playhouse offers an ambitious season of plays and musicals. Call (904) 255-2431 for ticket information.

DIRECTIONS

Take S.R. 430 East off U.S. 1 to Halifax. Turn left onto Halifax Drive to Jessamine Boulevard. The Daytona Playhouse is just off Halifax.

WALDO'S MOUNTAIN IN VERO BEACH

W*aldo Sexton was an entrepreneur* during the Florida land boom. He came to Vero Beach in 1913, and died there in 1969 at age eighty-two. During his lifetime he developed citrus groves, a packing house, and a dairy, among other concerns. Landmarks around Florida witness the impact he had on development. McKee Jungle Gardens, the Driftwood Inn (which expanded around a summer house he built for his family, and which displays many artifacts from his lifetime), and Ocean Grill Restaurant all owe their existence to Waldo Sexton. Much of the Vero Beach area is still in trust to the Sexton estate, including valuable waterfront land. His eccentric ways are legend and well-documented. He collected treasures and antiques to satisfy his artistic visions. Many of these came from wealthy Palm Beach residents who lost their holdings during the Depression.

The most daring and creative of Waldo Sexton's ideas was a mountain—a monument to himself, at which he wanted to be buried. Its height was not documented, but it must have been sizable, because the dirt from that mountain was moved, after his death, to save the Driftwood Inn from being eroded from years of storms along the coast. The mountain itself had steps going up the side, decorated with inlaid tile. On top were two chairs and a cross. He sat up there and viewed his holdings like a king. The pyramid-like monument was built on A1A, where the Ruddy Ducks Restaurant now stands. Locals remember climbing the steps of the mountain when they were young.

HAUNT HISTORY

Judy Martin, current owner of the Ruddy Ducks Restaurant, said it was, ironically, her husband who had moved the soil from the mountain, at the request of Ralph Sexton, Waldo's son, before Judy even owned the restaurant.

The previous owners were so haunted by Waldo's ghost that they asked a priest and later a psychic to free the restaurant of his spirit.

Ruddy Duck Restaurant

The psychic insisted that Waldo only wanted recognition. The previous owner, Loli Heuser, said that unexplained things happened. Glasses broke in her hand for no reason, pictures fell from the wall, and an image of Waldo himself was seen once. She planned to erect a miniature statue of him to appease him. Judy Martin said when she became the owner, she put up pictures of Waldo Sexton in the office. They are still there, along with a picture of Waldo's Mountain. In the restaurant a picture of Waldo is prominently displayed by the bar.

Evidently, the honor and recognition that Waldo Sexton wanted have been supplied by the present owner of the restaurant. There have been less frequent happenings, although occasionally Waldo reminds them of his mountain. Once a glass shattered in the bartender's hand as he was getting ready to prepare a drink. Another night, as the owners were closing up for the evening and after they had turned off the lights, they heard a big crash from the kitchen area. Thinking the whole pot rack had fallen, they went back and turned on the lights in the kitchen. Nothing was out of place. "We cannot keep batteries," Judy Martin said. "The remote that controls our music, flashlight batteries—the energy just seems to drain right out of them.

Waldo's Mountain

Even now we have difficulty keeping the batteries in flashlights. We've had other things happen, and I think, am I losing it? Other people would never believe this happened. There is something. . . ." Judy Martin said that when she and her husband leave the premises at night, they remember to say, "Good night, Waldo," or "Keep good care of the place, Waldo." "We don't forget him. I want to be on his good side," she said.

The restaurant is built in the form of a ship, with the prow extending out over the former site of Waldo's Mountain. When the lights that decorate the outline of the prow are switched on after dark, they seem to point up toward the top of Waldo's Mountain. He is remembered.

VISITING THE SITE

Even if you don't see Waldo's ghost when you visit the Ruddy Ducks, the food is worth the drive. The day I was there for lunch, snapper was the catch of the day. Broiled in lemon butter sauce, with perfectly cooked vegetables, it was an unforgettable lunch. Ask for a seat by the water. This restaurant is highly recommended. The Driftwood Resort, built around Waldo's beach house, displays many of Waldo Sexton's treasures, and villas in this time-share resort can be rented reasonably. It is located right on the water, on Ocean Drive.

DIRECTIONS

Take 60 East off I-95 to A1A. Turn north on A1A. Ruddy Ducks is on your left, at 4445 North A1A. Phone (407) 234-3880.

ASHLEY'S IN ROCKLEDGE

A*shley's Restaurant and Lounge* was opened in 1933, when Prohibition was fading into Florida history. Called Jack's Tavern then, it was an upscale restaurant and tavern, whose patrons wore tuxedos and evening gowns. Brevard County's first jukebox was installed in Jack's Tavern, and steaks cost less than $1. It was a successful venture for the owner, but in 1943 he was drafted and sold the restaurant. It was resold in 1946 and named Cooney's Tavern. Clayton Korecky's son inherited it and later sold it to Willie Schuhmacher, who renamed it the Mad Duchess. Three years later it was sold again, and called the Loose Caboose. Later Scott Faucher bought it, and sold it to Greg Parker, the present owner.

Ashley's Restaurant and Lounge is a large Tudor-style building constructed of wood and heavy beams. The quiet lounge area greets patrons entering from U.S. 1. Wood tables with comfortable chairs, set off by the dark wood walls, are reminiscent of an English pub. Sunlight streams in from skylights, furnishing light to the many plants that hang from the ceiling. Upstairs, the tables are placed around the railing, affording a view of the downstairs area. Businesspeople visit frequently for lunch, as it has a relaxing atmosphere. On football Mondays, it is a haven for sports fans, who gather in the lounge to enjoy the ninety-nine-cent drafts.

HAUNT HISTORY

"To be honest, I believe the place is haunted," former owner, Scott Faucher, volunteered. The incident he remembered most vividly happened when he was there late one night. He felt a "gust of wind" swish past him. Knowing that all the doors and windows were closed and the air conditioners were so far away from him, he could think of no logical explanation. "It was the most overpowering experience," he continued. Many times during his ownership, the police called him and reported lights on and movement inside. When they went in with dogs to check the place, they found nothing—no one. In March 1980, the Rockledge Police Department answered a call. The manager's office "looked like a tornado had hit it. There were papers and books scattered all over." The safe was open, but nothing had been taken, including some money. The RPD recorded it in their log book as "a suspicious incident."

Faucher said that employees avoided the storage rooms as much as possible because several of them had witnessed "incidents" there. A waitress named Arlene went into the storage room upstairs, and came down thoroughly shaken. She said she had seen a woman sitting at the desk. Another waitress, Marianne, said she went to the upstairs storage room for iced tea glasses. As she reached up, she extended her leg out for balance and kicked someone. She turned to apologize, but no one was there.

Cooks had their experiences, too. One morning a cook found bread baskets scattered all around his kitchen, after he had neatly stacked them the night before. George Heppler, another cook, said he saw a jar fly off the counter. Faucher and one of his cooks were preparing for lunch one day, and the exhaust fans, which were controlled by a switch twenty feet away, came on by themselves.

The ladies' room seemed to be a target for ghostly occurrences also. A customer came out of the ladies' room one time, screaming that the toilet had exploded. Sure enough, it was in several pieces. A female bartender was combing her hair in the ladies' room when the

Ashley's

Moving Pictures on Balcony of Ashley's

door opened. When no one came through the door, she thought she had better just leave. She pressed against the door to leave, but could not move it. When she pushed again, the door flew open.

Bartenders heard their names called, but when they turned, no one was there. Employees who had to work until closing paid other workers to stay late with them. Ted Innes, a tough-looking dishwasher with tattoos and a hefty build, was frequently chosen to stay late with his coworkers. One evening a piece of lemon flew out of the sink and across the room, but he said he was never afraid because he had never actually seen the ghost.

Two psychics were asked to investigate all the phenomena. They were convinced that more than one entity was haunting the restaurant, on different levels, which gave off confusing impressions. A lot has happened in the Tudor building. One of the psychics saw two uniformed men dragging a man down the stairs, with a young girl begging them to stop. At another session, the psychic saw a woman running downstairs, losing a lot of blood.

In 1934 a local newspaper reported the brutal murder of nineteen-year-old Ethyl Allen, a regular at Jack's Tavern. Her body was found on the shores of Indian River near Eau Gallie. There were conflicting reports about where she had last been seen. One of two possible places was Jack's Tavern. The body was mutilated, and only identified by a tattoo—a circle of rope around the initials "B. K."—on the right thigh just above the knee. It was reported she had been with a "well-dressed, nice-looking man." She was buried in Georgiana Cemetery on Merritt Island. The police never solved her murder.

In 1982 a photographer, Malcolm Denemark, was assigned to take pictures for an article being published in *Florida Today* about Gentleman Jim's, as the restaurant was then called. After developing the film, he saw an image of a man entering the lobby. No one had come in while he was shooting pictures. There was no shadow cast by the person, although other items in the picture had shadows. The photographer tried to recreate the scene, using a person where the image had appeared. The real person did cast a shadow. The *National Enquirer* bought the picture and ran an article about the restaurant. The *Ghostly Register*, a book published in 1986, contains an entire chapter on the restaurant.

Not knowing the entity's name—there may even be more than one—current employees simply refer to the strange goings-on as being caused by "Sarah." The unusual continues in Ashley's Restaurant and Lounge. Waitress Cathy Grant said that strange things go on continually. Pictures fall off the wall, five at a time, but are found the next morning lying neatly, face up and with no broken glass. Hurricane lamps are lit with no explanation.

Does the spirit of Ethyl Allen refuse to rest because her murderer was never caught? Or is the ghost possibly her murderer, returning to the scene of his ghastly crime?

VISITING THE SITE

Ashley's is open for lunch and dinner. The peel-and-eat shrimp are excellent, boiled in spices and served with hot bread. The locals insist that the salmon there is the best around. Rockledge is very near Cape Canaveral and the Merritt Island National Wildlife Refuge.

DIRECTIONS

Off I-95, take S.R. 520 to U.S. 1 and turn right. Ashley's is four miles on the right. Call (407) 636-6430.

CASSADAGA NEAR DAYTONA

Located on fifty-seven acres in Central Florida is a spiritualist camp called Cassadaga. Cassadaga derives its name from a word used by the Seneca Indians meaning "rocks beneath the water." Its founder, George P. Colby, was advised by one of his spirit guides, an Indian named Seneca, to establish a community in the South. Colby, following the instructions given to him during a seance, came to Blue Springs Landing, near Orange City, Florida. Later he was guided by his spirits through the wilderness to the site which is the present-day Cassadaga. The year was 1875. Although it was originally intended to be a winter place for spiritualists, many came to live as permanent residents. Most were well-educated and affluent, and they stayed in tents pitched on the grounds while cottages were being built. Some residents lived in Harmony Hall, a group of apartments which had been built on the grounds of the camp. Many built homes, and although they owned the homes in which they lived, the church owned the land and gave lifetime leases to the homeowners. This arrangement of leased land exists today.

Within the camp there are many beautiful spots for meditation. Seneca Park and a gazebo overlook Spirit Pond. A meditation garden with benches surrounds Centennial Fountain. Nature trails are prominent in the community, and Medicine Wheel Park is a place of peace honoring Native American Spirit.

The Cassadaga Spiritualist Camp celebrated its 100th birthday in 1994. It is designated a Historic District on the National Register of Historic Places. Mediums, spiritual healers, and teachers reside in Cassadaga, and visitors come from distant cities to seek guidance in this tranquil southern town. Spiritual counseling is obtained from a spiritualist minister or certified medium. (Certification may take anywhere from four to six years to acquire.). The medium's mind is used to receive, process, and deliver messages from those who have made their "transition." Black magic, witchcraft, and psychic tools such as palm reading and tarot cards are not used in the Cassadaga Spiritualist Camp, although palm readers are numerous within the town.

HAUNT HISTORY

The Cassadaga Hotel is said to be inhabited by Arthur, an Irish tenor who lived and died there in the 1930s. He turns the lights off and on to answer your questions, and visitors to Arthur's old room have said they smell cigars and gin. When I questioned the present hotel owners, they told me spirits are everywhere in Cassadaga. The whole town, in fact, is full of energy, because after all, Cassadaga is a spirtualists' camp.

The morning I was in Cassadaga, the hotel owners were very busy. The dining room was full of hungry customers, so I went outside to take a few photographs of this lovely hotel. I was able to take one shot, and the needle on the light meter on my camera began moving up and down rapidly. I tried to adjust the light, but it continued. I walked across the street and tried to take another picture. The needle continued its fast up-and-down movements. Not knowing much about cameras or light meters, I asked my sisters, who had come to Cassadaga with me, to look at it. The rapid movements continued, and finally I gave up taking pictures, believing that the battery was probably going bad. At home the next Monday, I took my camera in to the local camera shop, and told him I thought the camera needed a

Cassadaga

new battery. He looked at it, and said nothing was wrong—the needle was perfectly still. Then he checked the battery, and assured me it was fine. I have taken pictures since then, using the same battery, and the needle acted normally. Either Arthur did not want me to take a photograph of the hotel, or the spiritual energy in Cassadaga is truly so strong that it interrupts other energy sources.

I could not arrange a seance for that day, as appointments for these are made in advance. Even so, my trip to Cassadaga was a memorable one.

VISITING THE SITE

Visit the Camp Bookstore when you first arrive at Cassadaga. Current literature and schedules of camp activities are available here. There is a bulletin board where certified mediums sign in daily and a phone available to schedule readings with them. The Cassadaga Hotel and Clauser's Bed and Breakfast offer overnight accommodations. The camp phone is (904) 228-2880. Cassadaga Hotel is (904) 228-2323. Clauser's Bed and Breakfast is (800) 220-0310.

DIRECTIONS

Cassadaga is thirty-five miles northeast of Orlando and twenty-five miles southwest of Daytona, just off I-4. Take I-4 to Exit #54. Proceed to traffic light. Make a right turn onto C.R. 4101/Dr. Martin Luther King Jr. Beltway for approximately one quarter mile. Turn right at C.R. 4139/Cassadaga Road and drive about one and a half miles. Signs indicating Cassadaga Spiritualist Camp are on the right side of the road.

REGION FOUR

CENTRAL

MAITLAND ART CENTER

Just north of Orlando lies the small town of Maitland, built around many lovely lakes. The Maitland Art Center is a must-see for the haunt hunter and architecture buff. The artist Andre Smith (1880–1959) began building the art center on the shore of Lake Sybelia in the 1930s, and it was then called the Research Studio at Maitland. Smith was involved, both artistically and emotionally, with Aztec-Mayan themes, and the architecture at the center reflects this. He came to the United States from Hong Kong when he was ten years old. He studied at Cornell University and won prestigious awards throughout his career, one of which was a commission to design the Distinguished Service Cross. In 1937, the art center here was one of three art galleries in existence in Florida. It is a complete compound, housing artists, offices, classrooms, gardens, and exhibits. The highly decorated carvings are found at the entrances as well as throughout the grounds and chapel. It has a contemplative, old-world atmosphere, which draws exclamations of awe as visitors discover the beauty of the carvings.

HAUNT HISTORY

Numerous encounters with a "presence" have been reported by individuals directly connected with the art center. Smith's ghost has visited the potter artist-in-residence, James Cook, who received guidance and welcome feedback from Smith on his work. Cook heard conversations between Smith and a woman, discussing Cook's art. Smith's comments caused Cook to change the focus of his work, which led to a successful new approach. An Orlando medium, Dikki Jo Mullen, and other professional parapsychologists have investigated the presence which has made itself known since Andre Smith's death. Two reporters, while investigating these ghostly sitings, separately experienced a cold chill. This was in an area where Smith did his meditating. Visitors have smelled unexplained cigar smoke (Smith smoked cigars). The presence is felt more frequently from September to May (Smith traveled during the summer).

Maitland Art Center

At a wedding held, as many are, in the chapel, several people saw a figure behind the wedding party at the altar, dressed in an old-fashioned bridal dress. Later they were told that Smith had been obsessed by a bride. One appeared frequently in his paintings, once with a noose around her neck.

Bill Orr, another artist who lived at the center, also experienced Smith's presence. One evening as he was leaving the gallery, he heard glass breaking. He turned around and saw a transparent Smith. Orr ran out, slamming and locking the door behind him.

A receptionist once saw a rocking chair begin rocking by itself. The same receptionist several times heard pictures falling, but upon checking in the gallery found nothing disturbed. Tape recorders set at night have recorded tapping sounds. Schepp, the director, heard the tapping noises, a "thump-step, thump-step," after hanging a display of Smith's work, as if Smith himself were checking out the display. Smith had a wooden leg and sometimes used a crutch.

Some believe that because Smith was buried in Connecticut, so far from his life's work, his soul is restless. Others believe he is worried that the center will be torn down or changed. The simplest explana-

Wall at Maitland Art Center

tion may be Smith's own: in his will, he stated, "I will always be a presence here."

VISITING THE SITE

The Maitland Art Center presents lectures, children's painting workshops, exhibits, and classes throughout the year. It is listed in the National Register of Historic Places.

A few blocks south of the art center on 17-92 is the Bubble Room Restaurant, a very different place where you can relax and discuss your day. The decor is unique, with eye-catching memorabilia from the 1930s and 1940s. The food is great, and the restaurant is open seven days a week.

DIRECTIONS

Take Lee Road (Exit 46) east of I-4 until it dead-ends on 17-92. Turn left. At Packwood, turn left again. The art center is down a few blocks, on both sides of the red brick street. There are several signs to the center. Phone (407) 539-2181 for gallery and office hours.

POLASEK GALLERIES IN WINTER PARK

The *Polasek Galleries hold* two hundred sculptures and paintings done by Albin Polasek, a Czechoslovakian immigrant. The seventh son of a Moravian family, he was born on Saint Valentine's Day in 1879. This world-famous sculptor came to America in 1901, when he was twenty-two years old. He rode on a German ship in steerage class with other immigrants. According to his autobiography, when the ship landed in New York Harbor, he saluted the Statue of Liberty, whose uplifted torch symbolized to him the light of a new life.

Armed with nothing but his skills as a woodcarver, which he had acquired as an apprentice to a furniture maker in Vienna, Albin found employment carving frames and later religious carvings which now hang in a church at Veseli, Minnesota. His brother Robert was a priest in the parish of Veseli, and Albin stayed close to him as Robert was very ill. During this time, Albin became acquainted with his new country, and experienced for the first time new things not found in his homeland. Among these discoveries were round doorknobs: he had only used straight sticks to open doors in his native country.

Claiming to be an experienced figure sculptor, he obtained a position in an altar factory in Dubuque, Iowa, initially re-carving works that had not satisfied the buyer. His work, however, did please the buyer, and he gradually became known for his carvings. He was invited to work at a factory in La Crosse, Wisconsin. For three dollars a day, he carved angels. Later he worked by the piece, carving figures priced by the foot.

Albin dreamed of studying sculpture at the Pennsylvania Academy of Fine Arts in Philadelphia, and after a few years of factory work, he had saved enough money to study there. Later he was awarded the Cresson Foreign Traveling Scholarship. In 1910 he won a fellowship to the American Academy in Rome for his sculpture *Faith, Hope and Charity*, and studied in Rome for three years.

In 1916, Albin was asked to head the Department of Sculpture at the Chicago Art Institute. There he met art student Ruth Sherwood. She loved him for many years and even wrote *Carving His Own Destiny*, a book that chronicles his life. Albin, however, was in love with his art. *Carving His Own Destiny* is also the name of one of his most famous statues. It is the figure of a man chiseling himself from a block of marble. His statues of Daniel Boone and the famous *Mother Crying Over the World*, which he created during World War II, are in the Hall of Fame in New York City.

In 1950 he built his home and studio on Lake Osceola in Winter Park, using plans he had drawn.

Shortly afterward, he suffered a stroke. He continued to carve, using his one good hand. He finally married Ruth when he was seventy-two. She died eighteen months later following surgery for throat cancer.

After Ruth's death, Albin was cared for and visited by many old friends, including Dr. William Kubat and his wife Emily. Albin had known William since his early days in Chicago, and the two shared a Czech background. William died in 1960, and in 1961 Albin and Emily married. Together they decided to keep many of his "children," as he called his statues, at their Winter Park residence.

After Albin's death in 1965, a trust was established to care for his relatives in Moravia and for Emily. The remainder of his assets were left to a non-profit corporation, and from these assets the Albin Polasek Foundation was created. According to the epilogue in Ruth Sherwood's *Carving His Own Destiny*, Albin wanted his art to be seen and enjoyed by the

Tear on the Cheek of Jesus Sculpture at Polasek Galleries

public, free of charge, to express his appreciation to the American people for what their country had done for him.

Albin's last carving, *The Dream*, stands unfinished in a storage room, as the clay from which it was being carved is not stable enough for exhibition. A picture of it can be seen in the epilogue to *Carving His Own Destiny*, which was published in 1954 by Albin himself. His last painting, *Communion After the Last Supper*, was so large that Albin could reach only halfway up the canvas from his wheelchair. He had to turn the canvas and paint the upper half upside down.

HAUNT HISTORY

Just past the entrance gate to Polasek's home and the gallery is a bronze statue of Emily playing the harp, a wedding gift to her from Albin. Immediately the visitor is aware of Albin's profound talent. The spirit of this quiet retreat permeates every part of the gallery and grounds. Many locals believe Albin remains here with his sculptures, but the real sense of presence is that it is a spiritual place, a setting where meditation and renewal are imminent. Although Albin was a devout Roman Catholic, his works transcend religion, ideology, and nationality.

Margaret Moran, Managing Director of the Polasek Galleries, spoke of the profound effect the carvings and the chapel have on visitors. One day a visitor, Bill Sullivan, ran into Ms. Moran's office, demanding a camera. "We must take a picture of this. Where is a camera?" he insisted. He did manage to take a picture of the phenomenon: a tear on the cheek of Jesus at the *Stations of the Cross*, a group of carvings in bas relief. According to Ms. Moran, there was no explanation for its appearance. Mr. Sullivan, fearing that no one would believe them, asked Ms. Moran to get someone to witness the event. She ran to get a neighbor, and they sat on a bench near the display for several hours, watching, as the tear defied gravity. Finally it disappeared. The date was March 29, 1997, one day before Easter Sunday.

A huge oak on the grounds has lived decades beyond arborists' estimates of its lifespan. Many believe the reason is that it shelters a huge bronze crucifix, *Victorious Christ*, carved by Polasek.

One does not have to be knowledgeable of sculpture or art to appreciate the permeating beauty of this place. If possible, obtain some background information about a few of the statues before going there. Many of them are so powerful they remain in the mind's eye for days.

VISITING THE SITE

The Polasek Galleries are open Monday through Saturday from 10:00 A.M. to 4:00 P.M. Sunday hours are 1:00 P.M. to 4:00 P.M. The galleries are closed during July and August and on major holidays.

DIRECTIONS

From Interstate 4, take the Fairbanks exit east toward Rollins College. Fairbanks Avenue later becomes Osceola Avenue. The gallery is at 633 Osceola Avenue, across from the Rollins College campus. Phone (407) 647-6294.

INSIDE-OUTSIDE HOUSE IN LONGWOOD

Longwood, Florida, is listed on the National Register of Historic Places. In its early days, the town was one of the stops on the South Florida Railroad. Not to be outdone by its flashier neighbor, Orlando, Longwood quietly boasts of a unique history. As early as the 1880s, approximately one thousand residents lived here, their lives centered around the citrus and lumber industries. Longwood still retains the typical form that early Florida towns shared: a hotel with small cottages surrounding it, homes for permanent residents, churches, and a few stores.

The Inside-Outside House shares space with homes whose origins date to the 1880s. The house is one of the first examples of prefabricated buildings in the United States. It was built in the Boston area by Captain W. Pierce, a sea captain, around the year 1870. The framing structure was placed outside the exterior siding, forming panels which were then bolted together in ship-lap style. The studs and bolts can be seen on the exterior of the house, hence the name Inside-Outside House. In 1873, the unusual structure was disassembled and shipped to Jacksonville and from there to Sanford on a barge. Mule carts carried it twenty miles to Altamonte Springs.

After the house was reassembled in Florida, federal soldiers used it as a way station until its builder moved to Florida after retiring from the sea. He and his wife (and a favorite pet cat, Brutus) lived in the upstairs section. Pierce used the ground floor for a woodworking shop, making cabinets in his retirement years.

Before being moved to Florida, the house had only an outside staircase to the second floor, but Pierce built an interior circular staircase after he moved in. The staircase, still in the house, is a reflection of the captain's skill as a woodworker.

After Pierce's death, another family lived in the home, but eventually it was vacated and fell into disrepair. With land prices in Altamonte Springs rising, the house was considered for demolition, but was rescued by the Central Florida Society for Historic Preservation. The house was again moved, this time to Longwood. It is now leased as a gift shop and is open to the public.

HAUNT HISTORY

Brutus, the black cat, has been seen sitting in the upstairs window of the Inside-Outside House, looking at the passersby on the quiet street in Longwood.

Pamm Redditt shared information about her experiences in the house. When she first worked there, as an employee for a previous shop owner, she laughed at their stories of cats and unexplained happenings. But now that she is owner of the gift shop and spends long hours in the house, she has lost her skepticism. She's convinced that not only the cat but his master as well, the New England sea captain, remain there.

"I started working here in 1991, and bought the shop in 1995. The first sighting of Brutus was seen by previous owners and patrons. When I came I was very skeptical. Then one day, when I had been here about a year, something happened. I was upstairs, and all of a sudden, I felt someone was telling me I needed to be out of that room. I wasn't welcome. I bent over to pick up some paper bags, and suddenly I felt this very cold movement behind me, and cold all behind me, not just at my feet. Don't ask me why, but I immediately said aloud, 'I'm leaving this room now.' I walked out and closed the door. I was very nervous. There's no air conditioning in that room, so I knew it had to be something other than my imagination. Months later I was downstairs, and a woman was standing in the doorway between the front and middle rooms. She asked if I had the air conditioning on. I told her no, and she said she had just felt something very cold beside her. I said, 'Oh, really? Well, it must be a draft.' But I knew exactly what she had experienced, because it was the same feeling I had upstairs.

"The following summer, I was here by myself one day. A whole tray of merchandise that I was putting away just slipped out of my hand. The windows were closed, and the air conditioner was on. As I bent to pick up the items I had dropped, a very deep voice said 'Ye-e-s-s-s.' It was a very distinct voice, right behind me. I stood up as quickly as I could. I turned around and looked out the window. No one was there, and no one was in the shop. I was a nervous wreck. About a year later my sister came to visit, and I told her about that distinctive voice. She said, 'Pamm, that's ridiculous. It must have been someone outside.' So she went outside and talked to me, and I couldn't hear any of what she said.

"One evening during the winter, I went into the front room and turned off one of the lamps. When I turned around there was a silhouette of a man standing at the table near the front door. I immediately said, 'Oh, I'm leaving. I've been here long enough.' It scared me to death. Sometimes customers will say they have a funny feeling upstairs. I just think, I know.

"About nine months ago I was here working by myself, and I heard the front door open and close. It seems like early evening is always the time these things happen, as if I should be gone from the house by then. I thought it was my husband coming to help me, so I yelled down to tell him I was upstairs, and for him to come on up. There was no answer. So I said, 'Tom, I'm upstairs. That's not funny. Come on up.' There was still no answer. Thank goodness I had taken the portable phone up with me, so I called home and he answered. I told him what had happened, and that I wasn't leaving the upstairs until he came down to the shop. Someone, though, came into the house that night.

"The ladies who had the shop before me used to wear long dresses, and they said they sometimes felt a cat brush against them, and the sides of their dresses move. When I started working here, I thought what they told me was just a bunch of nothing. But after having experienced these things, I feel differently. And I'm really hesitant to tell anyone about it. My mother knows about the things that have happened, and she suggested I put a pot of annuals in one of the rooms, where I think the spirit is. If it's a good spirit, the flowers will live; otherwise they'll die. I told her I didn't want to know. I told my mother one morning, when she dropped me off at work, that I knew he wasn't a bad spirit, that he hadn't pushed me down the stairs or anything. Do you know, when I walked out the door that evening, I fell walking out the front door!

"I just really feel that the captain is in the house. I try to remember to greet him when I arrive in the morning and to say goodbye when I leave at night."

Another person who sensed the presence of a cat was Denni Manzullo, who was a young girl at the time. She was upstairs in the house, and when she entered the front room, the rocking chair gave a lurch as if something had jumped from it. She yelled out, and her father ran up the stairs just in time to see the chair still rocking. Denni declared then that the house was haunted. Many people attributed her story to the overactive imagination of a teenager. However, as an adult, Denni reported an actual sighting. As she was driving past the house one evening, she saw a light on in the back room upstairs. Then she noticed a black cat sitting in the window, clearly silhouetted by the light.

When Mary Anne Vandigriff and Angie Romaguso owned their shop in the house, many times they would return to find their silk flower arrangements scattered throughout the rooms, as if a cat had been playing with them.

Dorothy Giffin, the previous owner of the gift shop Culinary Cottage, stated that one day she heard scratching sounds inside the closet beneath the spiral stairs. When she opened the door, she saw nothing but felt something brush against her leg. Something came out, she insists: "I felt it."

Although Captain Pierce built Brutus a casket of teakwood, a sturdy and enduring wood prized by shipbuilders, it seems Brutus could not be contained within its ornate structure. He prefers instead to wander through the house built and occupied by his master. The old sea captain himself seems to have remained in the house, too, and he and his beloved pet perhaps enjoy reminding others that they are the real residents of this venerable old house.

VISITING THE SITE

Christmas in Olde Longwood, walking tours, an arts and crafts festival, and other scheduled events offer the visitor many ways to enjoy the town. Call (407) 332-0225 for information on Longwood's annual events. A sign in front of the Inside-Outside House identifies the house shared by the captain, his cat, and the Culinary Cottage. The Culinary Cottage is open Monday through Saturday from 10:00 A.M. to 5:00 P.M. Phone (407) 834-7220. Directly behind the Inside-Outside House, in the Browser's Barn, the Magnolia Tea Room offers a continental breakfast and lunch, and is open Tuesday–Saturday from 11:00 A.M. to 3:00 P.M. Phone (407) 331-1006.

DIRECTIONS

From I-4 take S.R. 434 East. Turn left onto 427. Turn left again onto Church Street. The Inside-Outside House is the third door on the left. From 17-92, turn west onto 434, then turn right onto 427 and left onto Church Street.

REGION FIVE

CENTRAL WEST

FORT COOPER STATE PARK NEAR INVERNESS

Wood ducks moved swiftly from the sawgrass that offered cover, and the lone sandhill crane waited for its mate to join him from across the Holathlikaha Lake, resenting my intrusion into their territory. Waterbirds and wildlife abound in this 710-acre park composed of hammock land and sandhill regions. The lake itself is spring-fed.

We can imagine how the spring lured first Seminoles to its banks and later a band of men who would try to drive out the Seminoles. Major Mark Anthony Cooper, heading the First Georgia Battalion of Volunteers during the Second Seminole War, stayed in this area to protect the sick and wounded who had to be left behind during General Winfield Scott's march to Fort Brooke in Tampa. Seminoles taunted Cooper's men from across the lake, attempting to get them to use their limited cannonballs, but Cooper was able to hold his own, and sixteen days later was relieved by Scott, who returned with reinforcements. The troops moved out, but the fort was later used as a post for U.S. Army detachments until the end of the war in 1842. The Seminoles, remarkably, were able to sustain small bands in and around the Cove of the Withlacoochee until the last few months of the war.

The state of Florida acquired the park from private owners in 1970. Excavations later confirmed the approximate size and shape of Fort Cooper. In 1977 it was opened as a state park.

HAUNT HISTORY

Steve Yosik, the park manager at Fort Cooper, pointed to a picture in his office. "Every time we have a controlled burn, this picture will lean. When I come in here after a burn, this picture will be crooked. I put this picture up across from it—of a chief—but it still happens." Yosik said he used to have a hut out back (since collapsed), but when he used it to barbecue, and lit the fire at night, he felt a presence around it. "Sometimes I said, 'Okay, Chief, it's lit—go for it.'" Yosik

View from Picnic Area at Fort Cooper

believes the "chief" likes fire. He knows the presence is a chief, but he does not know which one. "There are stories that there still is an old chief around here, to make sure things are kept in place. What his name is, nobody knows.

"We've had strange sensations back in the shop area. One of the rangers who lived back there felt the movement of both soldiers and Indians. We had a Seminole chief come from Tampa to see what he could see out here. Just sitting around my fire at night, I get a sense that there's someone around me. But my ex-wife has seen the chief. I had a small truck, and one day while out driving she said, 'He's dodging your truck right now!' I didn't see him. Sometimes the hair on my skin will just stand right up, and I'll say, 'Okay, enjoy the fire.'"

He interrupted the conversation to tell me that deer were being seen now that cooler weather had arrived. We also spotted raccoons and other wildlife as we drove through the trails in the park. "At the shop area, one of the rangers' wives saw him going through on horseback. Diana, another ranger, saw soldiers and Indians—back to back. She was only here temporarily, but she felt it all the time she was here, back in the shop area. My ex-wife knew the chief was even inside the

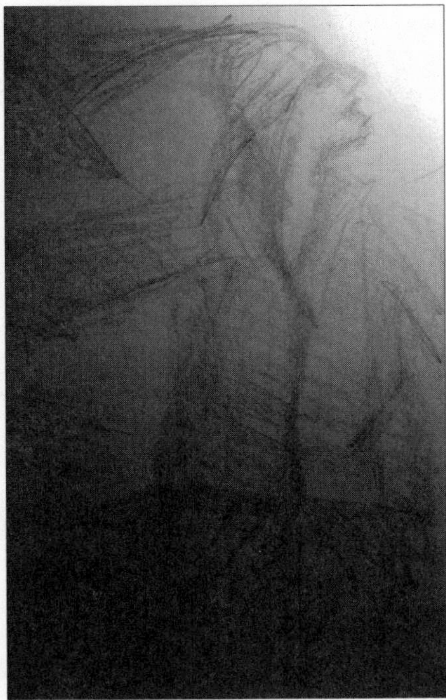

Sketch of Chief

Sketch of Chief

house. She had a chalk mark above the door to keep him out. The Indian is friendly. I think possibly he's still here because his tribe got wiped out here."

Lea Craig, a bright and charming Inverness resident, is a seventh-generation Floridian whose ancestors were Majorcans who came to Florida with the Spanish settlers. Lea lived at Fort Cooper from 1986 to 1994. "A lot of times people have such a vivid visualization, but with me, there was just a *knowing* that there was someone there. The more I opened myself up to it, the more I accepted the fact that there was something going on, the more certain I was about what I was feeling and experiencing. How can I be sitting here and talking about this? There is a fear that people are going to think you're off your rocker."

Lea explained that she and others had dubbed the presence "the chief," not really knowing who or what it was. She said her first experience at the park occurred one evening when she was reading. She looked up and sensed someone rushing toward the glass sliding doors. She felt anger in the spirit. At the time, the park manager worked on airboats, and it seemed the noise from the motors aroused the spirit's anger. "I first began my study on the park when I first became aware of the presence. The more educated I became about the kinds of things that happened—such as the Second Seminole War, a horrendous rout to get the Indians out of Florida because this is where white people wanted to be—the more I was aware." She got a horse, and many evenings would ride around the park. "A lot of times, particularly when I was out on the horse, by myself more often than not, I always had a sense that *he* was with me. I always had a sense that I was being watched after." She felt as though the spirit "was happy—glad that the horse was there" on the same paths the spirit walked in the park. "I went out one day and the horse heard a rattlesnake. She jumped out from under me, and I landed on my back in the sugar sand. The horse didn't bolt; she didn't run away. When that happened, I thought, 'I could have fallen on a tree stump—I could have broken my back.' I felt like I was being protected. There were times I was out in the evening and wouldn't get back until after dark. There is no light at the front gate—it was pitch black—but it was almost like coming home and having Dad waiting for you by the front door. I knew I was OK, and knew I was being looked after." Lea said she thought her children were "part of the attraction" the chief had for her.

At one time she had decided to look for the chief's burial place. During her first investigative walk, she developed a severe case of poison ivy, the first in all her life of living in Florida. The huge welts that rose on her arms made her decide to abandon the search. "It was like he was telling me, 'Leave well enough alone.' I never looked for his bones again."

Lea has made many sketches of the chief. Her sketches range from angry to sad, from resigned to peaceful. The earliest sketches all project anger. When she first moved into the house at Fort Cooper, she hated the backyard, the area in which she first sensed the chief's spirit of anger rushing toward her. She feels the chief was not sure he wanted her around. Later, as she became more accustomed to his presence, she planted lantana, beautyberry, and other native plants and became comfortable in the backyard area.

Frequently, Lea sketched the spirit at the lake. The annual reenactment at Fort Cooper in the spring reflects the ongoing skirmishes that were typical of what happened in the lake area. "It was more a harassment than an out-and-out battle, but it went on so long. It was the longest engagement of the Second Seminole War, because it continued daily for about sixteen days. I feel like it was not his intention to stay, that he was passing through."

Lea asked a card reader to go to the park to identify the chief, or whoever the spirit was. The reader said that this spirit was not a chief, rather an Indian who had been left in charge of a group of women and children, possibly to move them safely from one place to another. All were slain, and his spirit is not at rest because of this. He feels he failed at his assignment. "That's where the anger and sadness come from," Lea said, explaining her sketches.

VISITING THE SITE

Several small springs feed the lake at Fort Cooper, which is crystal clear due to what is commonly referred to as twice-filtered water. Besides a swimming area, the lake offers a fishing area and a playground. Rental canoes and paddleboats are available. Two primitive campsites, designed to hold about four or five tents each, remain fully occupied during the winter months. The park takes reservations only three months in advance for the sites, but they are well worth the wait. This is a popular site for Boy and Girl Scout groups.

Fort Cooper Days are held every April, when "Seminoles" and "Army regulars" reenact skirmishes and go about their daily chores in authentic settings. There are nearly five miles of self-guided nature trails in Fort Cooper. Weddings and seminars are held in an enclosed pavilion that sits among giant oak trees. A fireplace at one end makes the pavilion an ideal setting for celebrations.

DIRECTIONS

From U.S. 41 in Inverness, turn east onto Eden Drive. Follow the directional signs to Fort Cooper.

THE TAMPA THEATER

In *the middle of Tampa* sits what is called "the most beautiful theater in Florida." It is a tribute to the glory days of Hollywood, when movie palaces carried the viewer into a land of starry skies, ballroom dances, and happy endings. The theater opened in 1926 with a showing of the silent movie "Ace of Cads." Tickets were seventy-five cents, and flappers lined up to see the newly built movie theater. The architect was John Eberson, who had a reputation for the dramatic, both personally and professionally. He was frequently seen dressed in a top hat and cape, eccentric even in that era. Although he designed more than fifty theaters, the one in Tampa was always his favorite. In his words, he designed the theater "from the color and design . . . in the flowers and the trees." In the ceiling were tiny lights that flickered with varying intensity, simulating twinkling stars. Clouds billowed across his "sky," and the theatergoer was transported to a starry garden. The architecture, while predominantly Baroque, has elements of Spanish and Italian-Renaissance, a style referred to as "Florida-Mediterranean." Statues are prominently displayed around the theater, and Christopher Columbus stands among Greek and Roman mythological figures. Antiques furnish the hallways, and water fountains adorned with cherubs offer drink to patrons. On many evenings, gardenias are floating in the basins, a holdover from earlier times.

In 1973, the theater became a financial burden, and the owners offered to sell it to the city. Fortunately, Tampa officials appreciated the historical significance and the beauty within, and in 1977 reopened the theater after a massive restoration project. It is open year-round and shows foreign films and classics, as well as hosts live concerts and special events. The Mighty Wurlitzer is still played at the beginning of each film, and we are reminded that going to the theater is a way of living in another world—where the night skies hold only stars and billowy white clouds.

The Tampa Theater is now managed by the Arts Council of

Tampa Theater

Hillsborough County. It is listed in the National Register of Historic Places, and is a member of the League of Historic American Theaters.

HAUNT HISTORY

Foster "Fink" Finley came early and stayed late. He rode the bus to work, arriving hours earlier than necessary. The projection booth was his home away from home. He kept a shaving kit there, and he read the morning paper in the early hours before other workers arrived. When the theater opened in the afternoon, Finley and another projectionist ran the two projectors, bringing to life the stars of Hollywood's Golden Age.

In 1965, a very ill Finley was taken from the projection booth. Two months later, he died. Bill Hunt, the last projectionist to work with Finley, said he has since witnessed Finley's presence. "I went upstairs one day through the generator room, one of two entrances to the booth. I went through the door and somebody pulled back on the door. I looked back and nobody was there. That was really a strange feeling," he said. Another theater employee of eighteen years, Syd Morris, recalled that some projectionists refused to work there because of the eerie happenings. He recalled a time the power shut off while a worker was away from the power switch. The switch was "pretty snug as a rule," and it was after that incident that a projectionist was "ready to leave."

Angel Alturzarra has perhaps had the most contact with Finley's ghost. He once saw "somebody in white sitting in the theater" when it was supposed to be empty. Once his buck knife vanished. He looked everywhere for it, and then remembered Finley's ghost. He walked upstairs toward the projection booth and said, "Ghost of the theater, please return my knife." "I walked around the corner and there it was, leaning sideways against the wall." Once, a seance was planned in the projection booth to try to contact Finley's ghost. Alturzarra was mulling over the possibility of a seance and suddenly "all the lights turned on for about two seconds. I heard 'click, click.' It was the transformer kicking in. How could it do that? I perceived it as a warning from Fink that he didn't want the seance." In a third-floor shower, water was heard running. When Alturzarra went up, it was off. He left, and it came back on. He tightened the fixture, and when he left, it flowed again. "This stuff doesn't happen to me anywhere but this place," he said.

Tara Schroeder, the theater's public relations manager, said that a worker who came in early one morning heard keys rattling. He called out, thinking it was the custodian, but there was no response. Schroeder says although this worker said he needed "proof" before he could believe in ghosts, he nevertheless was convinced he had "encountered a poltergeist." Tara herself is convinced. As she accompanied a parapsychologist around the theater several months ago, the tri-field meter he was using to detect electromagnetic waves "went nuts." The waves were the type associated with ghost phenomena. Patrons have reported seeing an apparition float across the screen during the showing of a film.

VISITING THE SITE

The Tampa Theater is a must-see for visitors near the Tampa Bay area. The opulence is unparalleled in the few theaters of this caliber that remain. The Caffé Firenze is located a few doors from the theater. Have lunch and one of their homemade desserts before your theater event. It will be an unforgettable afternoon. For theater information call (813) 274-8286, or write P.O. Box 172188, Tampa, FL 33672. Caffé Firenze can be reached at (813) 228-9200.

DIRECTIONS

Take Downtown Exit #25 off I-275. Follow Ashley Street four lights south to Zack Street. Turn left on Zack. Go two blocks to Franklin Street (pedestrian mall). Tampa Theater is on the left at 711 Franklin Street. Street meters are free after 6 P.M. Monday through Friday and all day on weekends. Take quarters for parking during the week, or use one of several parking facilities near the theater.

CENTER PLACE IN BRANDON

W*hen the Depression hit Florida*, the area east of Tampa, known as Brandon, was farmland and orange groves. The eastern part of Brandon was mostly chicken houses, where growers raised poultry to take to the Latins in Ybor City, who would not buy iced or frozen birds. The town's growth began in the 1940s as a bedroom community of Tampa. Brandon's phenomenal expansion culminated in the 1980s, when the population grew by 61 percent. The town now has 116,415 residents.

Situated in the southwestern part of town is the Brandon Cultural Center, known as Center Place. The site overlooks a lake, and the wooden deck around Center Place hovers near the water, banked by water flowers. Signs alert visitors that it is an environmentally sensitive area. Originally the Cultural Center stood by itself on the prop-

Center Place

erty, but in 1991 it was rebuilt and enlarged. The Brandon Library is now in an extension of that building.

HAUNT HISTORY

Matilda is shy and appears quietly, dressed in blue. Dick Cimino, a former Center Place board member and Brandon businessman, was quoted as saying "something weird is indeed happening" when he glimpsed a young girl's form while answering a building security check. He continued with a description of the ghost, who momentarily froze as she was spotted in the light, then disappeared. Cimino checked every room, but could find nothing. "I would swear I saw something," he insisted. Cris Pacetti, a former Center Director, said that she has sensed movement but has never actually seen Matilda. "I just sense a presence," she said. Artists have told of paintings being moved at unexplained times during exhibits there. According to Gale Ruth, Center Place coordinator, rebuilding the Cultural Center has not discouraged Matilda. Upon completion of the new building, newspaper reporters came to do an article on the new Center Place. When they began asking questions about Matilda, the lights began to flicker, interrupting their interview. Speculation as to the origin of the ghostly presence abounds, but most observers think she is just a long-gone art lover who wants to be near artists.

VISITING THE SITE

Brandon is a shopper's dream. Brandon Town Center, just off I-75 on Rt. 60, is one of the largest malls in Florida. Center Place offers children's and adult art classes, as well as live dinner theaters and candlelit evenings of cabarets in the three-hundred-seat auditorium. Call ahead and plan to be there for a concert or drama production. Phone (813) 685-8888, or write Center Place, 619 Vonderburg Drive, Brandon, FL 33511-5210.

DIRECTIONS

From I-75 take S.R. 60 east to Brandon. Go through eight traffic lights from I-75 and turn right onto South Parsons Avenue. Go three blocks to Vonderburg Drive. The large Center Place building is visible from the intersection of South Parsons and Vonderburg.

JOHNS PASS AT TREASURE ISLAND

T*he bridge at Johns Pass* connects the more northern of the gulf beaches with Treasure Island, bound on the east by Boca Ciega Bay and on the west by the Gulf of Mexico. To get a good view of the water, park in front of any of the shops that line the entrance to the boardwalk. Small stores, fronted with weathered wood, line the walk on the land side, and on the bay side are numerous sea birds, drawn there by regular feedings.

There is disagreement among historians as to the nationality of the man for whom the pass was named. His last name has been spelled Lavach, Levique, and Levick. He was a turtle hunter, and evidently

Johns Pass Boardwalk

spent most of his time near the area now known as Johns Pass. The original bridge was built in 1927. I remember it well. My father remodeled the Kingfisher Restaurant, which was a popular dining spot for locals and visitors. It was the favored seafood spot for family celebrations. After the current bridge was built in 1971, west of the old one, the Kingfisher closed.

HAUNT HISTORY

In 1862, brothers Scott and John Whitus were returning to their Seminole home after having sailed to Egmont to obtain food for their families. Because they were considered Federal sympathizers, their Confederate neighbors had turned on them, and they were forced to ask for food and protection at Egmont, a federal outpost. As they were approaching Johns Pass, they were ambushed and killed by Southern sympathizers. Their bodies were buried near the pass.

The Whitus brothers' spirits have been seen in and above the waters around Johns Pass, going to and from their Seminole homesite.

Sometimes fishermen on the bridge have seen the ghosts gliding across the bay. Visitors to the boardwalk have seen them, explained away by unbelievers as phosphorescent bubbles or neon light reflections. If you are on the boardwalk after dark, look down into the water and across the bay: you may see their restless spirits near the bridge or in the depths of the bay.

VISITING THE SITE

Be sure to take your camera, because the pelicans will land within a foot of you, sometimes to preen and sometimes just to stare back at your camera lens. A two-hour cruise ($12 per person) takes visitors to other shores on the bay, affording a view of dolphins and numerous seabirds. The Friendly Fisherman Restaurant, on the boardwalk, serves wonderful grouper sandwiches. The restaurant is aptly named, as the employees keep an eye out for injured seabirds and call the Seabird Sanctuary for frequent rescues.

DIRECTIONS

Take the Madeira Beach Causeway from St. Petersburg to Gulf Boulevard South. Turn left at the Boardwalk sign at Johns Pass. The shops are open seven days a week. To book the cruise, call (813) 398-6577.

REGION SIX

SOUTHWEST

BOCA GRANDE LIGHTHOUSE ON GASPARILLA ISLAND

C*rossing the bridge onto Gasparilla Island* is a feast for the soul. Seabirds whirl overhead as if guarding the bobbing fishing boats. The island is a microcosm of Florida: huge, tiled-roof estates on the water, modest 1950s-built block homes, yachts, and native fishermen in small boats. Gasparilla Island is one of a chain of barrier islands on the Gulf coast of Florida, separated from the main peninsula by Charlotte Harbor and Pine Island Sound. In early days, Calusa tribes, whose presence is documented by small mounds on the island's north end, came there for the fish, turtles, and shellfish in the waters.

Swimming in the Gulf of Mexico and saltwater fishing in the deep waters of Boca Grande Pass bring visitors year-round. Shelling, though, is best during the winter months. Two picnic areas are located in the park, one at the northern end of the island, the other at the southernmost point adjacent to the lighthouse. Both spots offer panoramic views of the surrounding water. The atmosphere and friendliness of the permanent residents are reminiscent of the Florida Keys, in spite of the lavish Palm-Beach-type residences clustered along the water.

At the southernmost end of Gasparilla Island, in the Gasparilla Island State Recreation Area, stands a wooden lighthouse. It now serves as headquarters for park rangers, and the U.S. Coast Guard operates the light. One of the rangers lives in the assistant keeper's house.

Originally named the Charlotte Harbor Light Station, the lighthouse was built in 1890 on land that was then part of a military reservation. When a phosphate plant was built at the southern end of the island, ships came from all over the world to load. The lighthouse then became a critical navigational aid for mariners coming into Port Boca Grande. In 1927 the Coast Guard built a taller lighthouse (Rear Range Light) a mile and a half from the old lighthouse and moved the

Boca Grande Lighthouse

Fresnel lens to the taller lighthouse. During the next two decades, the old lighthouse stood abandoned. At one point, due to erosion around the piers on which it stood, it almost fell into the sea. In 1971 the government deposited thirty-five thousand cubic yards of sand at strategic locations around the lighthouse, which had now been turned over to the General Services Administration by the U.S. Coast Guard. The following year, Lee County obtained ownership of the lighthouse, and the precarious tilt of the building was corrected. In 1980 it was placed on the National Register of Historic Places. Since then, through grants and citizens' contributions, the lighthouse has been lovingly restored, and the Coast Guard reinstalled the third-order lens and recommissioned the old lighthouse as operational.

HAUNT HISTORY

The old lighthouse and surrounding area have seen many tragedies—and many ghostly visitors. Ranger Dave Porter, who grew up nearby, related the tale of José Gaspar. "He kept all his captive women down at Captiva. That's where the island gets its name. Gaspar brought his special one, Josefa, up here onto the beach. This is where she refused his advances, and he cut off her head with his sword and took the head back to his ship as a memento. The headless woman wanders the beach looking for her head."

He continued: "Between 1890 and 1910, either the first or second assistant was so lonely he committed suicide in the assistant keeper's house, next to the lighthouse."

Michael Cohorn, one of the rangers at the lighthouse , related his personal experience with perhaps the saddest unexplained "presence": "One of the keepers by the name of McKinney had a little girl who died of a fever. Once I was in the other room, and I had left the door open. I heard humming coming from the room where the lighthouse keeper's offices used to be, facing the water. But there was no one here. The receptionist and the assistant lighthouse keeper have heard her playing jacks. They can hear the ball bouncing, and she'll throw the jacks, up on the second floor of the lighthouse."

VISITING THE SITE

A toll drawbridge ($3.20) crosses the water to Gasparilla Island. Honor parking ($2) is observed at the park. The lighthouse has an interesting display of shells, including turtle shells and an empty turtle egg. The taller lighthouse, which for a time housed the lens from the old lighthouse, is on the right as you go south toward the Boca Grande Lighthouse.

In town, the Temptation Cafe has a very modest exterior but don't pass it by. The waitress knows everyone, because it is where all the locals eat. The grouper sandwich would make anyone come back, and the ample servings in a serene, quaint setting are not what one expects beyond the unpretentious screen doors. Fish recommendations are changed according to the catch and weather. Call (941) 964-2610 for reservations.

DIRECTIONS

Take I-75 to River Road (Exit 34), which later becomes C.R. 775. Follow the signs to Boca Grande.

CABBAGE KEY INN

Overhead, *ospreys catch the wind* currents and escort the launch that takes visitors from Pine Island to Cabbage Key. Nothing ever changes here. Mary Roberts Rinehart built the place in the 1930s as an island hideaway, and that it still remains. It is truly a retreat so remote, it is only accessible by boat. Because of limited access, the shelling is rewarding. The island has an elegantly shabby fish-camp atmosphere, and the inn sits atop a Calusa shell mound. The inn has six guest rooms, and there are six cottages perched among the oaks and mangroves. Day visitors may come from Bokeelia on Pine Island for lunch at the inn, and boaters from the Intracoastal Waterway are frequent guests at the inn's restaurant, which is said to have inspired Jimmy Buffett's tune, *Cheeseburger in Paradise*. This truly is paradise for those who enjoy getting away from all the popular attractions. Taking a day trip to nearby Cayo Costa, or spotting porpoises, is as exciting as it gets. It is what has been called a "power place," where one can renew the soul and spirit.

HAUNT HISTORY

Judy Natale, the general manager of Cabbage Key Inn, talked to me about the persistent stories that circulate about the inn. "I have personally witnessed one incident. The rest are incidents that have been told to us repeatedly over the years by guests who have stayed here. These are people who don't know each other, yet we find that year after year we hear the same stories. The guests who report these things to me are generally older people. They're not 'partiers'; they're not people who stay in the bar late. They go to bed early.

"The story I hear over and over is that a woman comes through the screen porch door—there's a little porch attached to that room. She has a blue skirt, a black belt, and a white blouse with long sleeves, and she has long, brownish hair. She just comes in, walks around, and sits down on the couch or stands next to the bed. She never stays long—half an hour maybe—then she strolls out the door into the hall without opening the door. None of the guests who saw her ever said they were afraid; it's more a curiosity than anything else. She doesn't speak, even when someone speaks to her.

"We're a little chain of islands here. There was a doctor who traveled around in his boat and treated people on these islands. Well, his wife would come here for lunch about twice a year. She told us that the Rinehart family had a houseguest who was recovering from tuberculosis. She was from New York. She was in her mid-thirties, and she had two small children. She was sent here to recover. Her husband saw her repeatedly through a winter, and in the spring, the woman became ill, came down with pneumonia, and died. The doctor's wife doesn't remember if the woman stayed in that room, but she was over on that side of the building. The rooms were set up at that time like a suite. There are six guest rooms now that used to be three suites. One of the bedrooms was set up like a parlor, and the other was set up like a bedroom.

"We've always heard a lot about that lady. I have spoken to people who were the caretakers here during the fifties, and they came here without children. The woman told me she made bread. She put the yeast mix on the table, and she turned around, and it was on the floor. She thought she had bumped it, so she picked it up, dusted it off, and put it back on the table. She took two steps and it was on the floor again. So she put it on the table, put a bowl over the top, and walked away from it. The bowl went flying across the kitchen and the dough wound up on the floor. She gave up bread making for that night, but she said the next day she was making bread again in that same area. Her husband put a bowl on top of the dough and he put a brick on top of the bowl. The brick went through the window, the bowl smashed on the floor, and the dough went on the floor too. So she said she just persisted, and that whole first summer it just drove them crazy, but after that it never happened again. She felt it was some spirit that just didn't like change. She felt that every time they changed or moved anything, some strange event would occur.

"Once, one of the servers and I were in the main dining room. Nobody else was here, and we were talking, having a cup of coffee, just standing, and there was a table between us. On it there was an empty tub used to carry dishes from the tables to the kitchen. The bus tub shot off the table. It went clear across the room. We didn't know what to do. It was the most amazing thing you've ever seen in your life. It flew twelve feet, hit the wall, and banged down onto the floor.

"A couple of the owners of this place—struggling young business people—told me about when they first bought it. They were keeping all their money in a little basket. As she was getting ready to leave and lock up the bar, she turned around and the money was gone. It was in the next room. This happened over and over. She got so annoyed one night she just came out into the middle of the dining room and said to the thin air in front of her, 'You cut that out!' It never happened again."

The ghost who frequents the Cabbage Key Inn is generally believed to be the restless spirit of the young woman who died there after contracting tuberculosis in New York. Is she looking for her absent family, or does she just enjoy keeping things stirred up at the inn? Cabbage Key is such a lovely piece of Florida—perhaps the explanation is that she simply wants to remain on the island.

VISITING THE SITE

Day-long cruises offer trips to all of Lee County's offshore coastal islands. Half-day trips are also available to take lunch guests to Cabbage Key. If you are staying at the Cabbage Key Inn, a water taxi is available for transportation from Pine Island and Captiva Island to Cabbage Key. Marinas on Pine Island also offer varied itineraries to the islands. If staying at Cabbage Key Inn, picnic lunches and trips to nearby Cayo Costa State Park can be arranged. Rates at the inn vary seasonally. Call (941) 283-2278 for information. The restaurant is noted for its wallpaper of autographed $1 bills, and boaters frequently stop in just for the seafood.

DIRECTIONS

Cabbage Key Inn can be accessed only by boat. From the Intracoastal Waterway, head west at Mile Marker 60.

PALM COTTAGE IN NAPLES

D*uring the end of the nineteenth century*, Naples was still a well-kept secret, a place where northern industrialists could get away from the cold weather without going to Miami or West Palm Beach, which already had the busy social schedules that accompanied the fast-growing tourist resorts. In 1895, Walter Haldeman, publisher of the *Louisville Courier Journal*, acquired a large parcel of prime land in Naples, Florida. He purchased the pier, the Naples Hotel, a sloop and steamer, a house, and 8600 acres of land for $50,000. He then built a two-story house which would later be called Palm Cottage. Originally intended to handle guest overflow from the Naples Hotel, it eventually became a home for his editor, Henry Watterson. Now owned by the Collier County Historical Society, it is one of the few remaining homes in southwest Florida which was constructed using tabby mortar.

Watterson lived in the house from 1895 to 1912. The serene setting encouraged him to pen many editorials from the library of Palm Cottage. His articles were then taken to the pier a few blocks down the road and sent to Fort Myers, where they were telegraphed to the *Louisville Courier Journal*. When writing of Naples, he spoke of the ample venison, pompano, and oysters he enjoyed from this pristine part of Florida: ". . . to the fisher and the hunter, Naples is virgin; the forest and the jungle about scarce trodden, the waters, as it were, untouched." Watterson later was awarded the Pulitzer Prize for one of his editorials which supported the entry of the United States into World War I. Literary talent ran in the family. His cousin was Samuel Clemens—Mark Twain.

Walter Palmer was the next owner, and the one who gave Palm Cottage its name. He sold it to two Canadians in the 1930s. In the 1940s, Laurance and Alexandra Brown bought the house. During their ownership, the house was visited by motion picture stars including Gary Cooper, Robert Montgomery, and Hedy Lamarr. It is told that when Brown raised the cocktail flag, the entire community knew that it was party time at the Brown's. After her husband's death,

Alexandra Brown remained at Palm Cottage until her own death in 1978.

During Hurricane Donna in 1960, much of Naples was devastated, and Palm Cottage did not escape the wrath of this terrible storm. It was flooded with hurricane tides, but the Browns, along with others who had endured Donna's punishment, cleared the debris and dried out their belongings. Following the cleanup of the town, Naples began experiencing a growth spurt.

HAUNT HISTORY

Fritzi Ryan, the Executive Director of Collier County Historical Society, shared a few stories about the strange happenings in the old house. "I've been here about three years. At first it was business as usual." She explained that restoration began about a year after she arrived. The cost of the restoration ran over four-hundred thousand dollars. "Two of the carpenters working on the restoration continually reported that their tools were moved. They didn't get upset, but just found them and began work again. The workers also experienced cold spots, particularly in the hallway. And what is interesting is that the Browns usually centered their lavish parties in that hallway. I've noticed things, too. Things have been moved around. There's no doubt in my mind that spirits exist, and I think there is a nice spirit here." She explained that Laurance Brown was considered an outcast by his wealthy family in Pittsburgh, who supplied him with an allowance to live in Naples. "So he and his wife just lived here and gave parties and enjoyed life," she explained. He had gone to Yale, she said, and had been in the Marines during World War II, but evidently there was some reason his family ostracized him.

Ms. Ryan continued: "There was a house next door, on the east side. The owners left one evening and their fourteen-year-old son stayed home. It seems he was smoking, and fell asleep, burning down the house. The fire spread to the upstairs part of this house, essentially burning most of the top story. The boy was killed in the fire. I don't know if he is the spirit." While the misplaced tools and articles may be the work of a young boy, it is also likely that Alexandra Brown, who with her husband spent happy years there entertaining celebrities, has remained in the old house and still moves quietly through the rooms, fingering her piano and placing things where she thinks they should be kept.

VISITING THE SITE

Tours of the house are given Monday through Friday from 1:00 P.M. to 4:00 P.M., except on legal holidays. There is no fee, but a $5 donation is requested. Group tours can be arranged by calling (941) 261-8164. After the tour, take the one-block walk to the Naples Pier and enjoy the calming breeze from the water. When the Gulf air has given you an appetite, go to Trio's Restaurant, just across 3rd Street. Nestled among a gallery of shops, the restaurant is easy to locate because of its bright blue umbrellas.

Trio's menu offers a wide selection of Mediterranean dishes. Try the half-salad with grilled shrimp and scallops, dressed with a light vinaigrette. The friendly waitresses bring a basket of thin-sliced hot bread to your table with your beverage. Hours are 11:00 A.M.–10:00 P.M. Monday through Saturday, with lunch being served daily until 4:00 P.M. Sunday hours are 5:00 P.M.–10:00 P.M. from November through May. Trio's is closed on Sundays during the summer. Phone (941) 649-8333.

DIRECTIONS

From I-75 take C.R. 896 west to U.S. 41 South. Go to 5th Avenue South and turn right. At 3rd Street, turn left and go to 12th Avenue South. Turn right and park under the big trees. Palm Cottage is at 137 12th Avenue South. Trio's Restaurant is just east of the house at The Plaza, across 3rd Street and up the steps.

REGION SEVEN

SOUTHEAST

JONATHAN DICKINSON STATE PARK (TRAPPER NELSON) NEAR JUPITER

The dark slow-moving waters of the Loxahatchee River in its wild and scenic setting seem unchanged since being fished by Florida's earliest inhabitants. Sunning turtles slip lazily from a log and splash into the river's dark cover. Alligators sun themselves on the banks, undisturbed. Cypress trees, decades old, stand nearby, watching the river.

Vince (Trapper) Nelson arrived in Florida riding on top of a freight train. He had traveled throughout the United States and Mexico. At one time he was held in a Mexican prison on a gun-running charge but was released for lack of evidence. During the Depression, he bought Florida land at tax sales. He was a large, well-built man, six feet four inches tall, who lived a solitary life on the Loxahatchee. At his death, the eight hundred acres he owned were bought by the state for Jonathan Dickinson Park, which is twenty percent coastal sand pine scrub, a biological community so rare it is designated "globally imperiled." The camp has been restored to its original condition so park visitors can enjoy the legend that Trapper Nelson left behind on the Loxahatchee.

HAUNT HISTORY

Park Ranger Cheryl Wells gave me a tour of Trapper Nelson's property. The tour starts at the boat dock. She said everything was just as it was when Trapper was here, with the exception of a few items such as the water fountain, the display case, and the benches down by the boat dock. "Trapper was the kind of man who lived life on his own terms, and did what he wanted to do."

Trapper Nelson had moved to Jupiter in 1929 and set up a homestead near the lighthouse. Then people started moving in, the animals started dying off, and he moved up the river. First he built a chickee, a minimal shelter inspired by those built by the Seminoles, to give him some protection while he was building. Trapper had no electricity; he used only hand tools to cut and size the logs to build his cabins.

Trapper was an eccentric man who usually wore shorts and tied a bandanna around his head. He used to swing out over the river on a rope tied to a big cypress tree, surprising tour boat parties from Palm Beach. After landing in the water, he would swim over to the boat and negotiate the cost of local docking. He exhibited snakes for money, and kept animals in cages like a small zoo. He also sold fruit from trees on the property.

When I asked Cheryl about the ghost who haunts the property, Cheryl said, "I'll be doing a tour, like now, and he's definitely here. Quite often it happens when I'm talking about his death. I get goose bumps and my hair stands on end. Sometimes I sense him when I'm coming out and waiting for the people. His body was found underneath the chickee. Sometimes, when I first arrive in the morning and I'm setting up, I'll feel anger and I'll think, 'What did I do?' It's as if he doesn't want any company.

"The first week I was out here, I was training with another ranger. He and I were taking a break, and I *felt* Trapper—I felt him and he was talking to me, and he said, 'If I weren't dead, I'd be asking you out.' I looked at the ranger and asked him if Trapper was a little bit of a lady's man. He looked at me and said, 'How did you know that?' I told him what had just happened and said, 'He's here, and he's flirting with me.'

"At our headquarters in the park I was going through the interpretive files, and I read the file about Trapper. There was a picture of him with a six-foot diamondback rattlesnake. As I was thinking about him, he just showed up there. Jan was in her office, but I didn't say anything. I just looked at him and acknowledged him, and I got the impression that he was ticked off. The coroner's report said his death was ruled a suicide. I heard a rumor when I was a kid that he took his shotgun, latched it down through the chickee railing, and pulled the trigger with a string. There are all kinds of rumors about how he died."

She went on to relate another rumor that another trapper was murdered by Trapper's brother. Trapper testified against him in court, and his brother swore vengeance. Another story goes that some men went out to rob Trapper, as it was thought that he had a great deal of money stashed out there. "But . . . killed himself? No, I don't think so. The shotgun was found too far from the body for the natural recoil of a shotgun. He didn't kill himself because his traps were still open. He respected the animals that he made his living from too much to leave his traps open. One of the boat captains told me that some lady had gotten off the boat, grabbed hold of a tree, and said, 'Somebody was murdered out here!'"

She said Trapper had married, and when he went into the military his wife left. When he returned, he found her waitressing in a Jupiter restaurant, but they never got back together. He didn't marry anyone else. The only relatives he claimed were a niece and nephew. Trapper's ashes were thrown in the river.

She interrupted our discussion about Trapper to show me two large gopher tortoises, one sitting on top of a sand mound. Both watched us, unafraid, as we passed them on the path.

"Maybe he feels there's some unfinished business, something that needs to be done before he can move on. I've heard him sometimes, asking me for help. 'What do you want me to do?' I ask. What it is, I don't know. That's why I'm having the psychics come out. I told them, 'I believe he wants me to help him.' Or it might be the Seminole Indians out here who need help. I don't know."

In the evening, the sounds of someone tramping through the woods, and sometimes a voice near the old cabin Trapper built, have been heard. "You hear it, and it almost sounds like a voice, almost makes you think someone is there," said Bob Schuh, another ranger. Schuh explained that when park workers were restoring the cabin, they found a loose brick at the fireplace, and unearthed over five thousand coins from Trapper's hiding place. All the time the workers were retrieving the coins, which took almost forty-five minutes, two ospreys circled overhead, at times taking dives toward the cabin and screeching. What was surprising about the incident is that ospreys usually hunt quietly. The unusual occurrence made Schuh feel uneasy. He said that it was as if the rangers had discovered Trapper's hiding place, and he was up there watching. The money—not quite two thousand dollars—was turned over to the Division of Historical Research in Tallahassee. The division records such findings and deposits them in the appropriate storage facility under the direction of the Bureau of Archaeological Research.

On a cool fall evening, we met at the picnic area for the boat ride to Trapper Nelson's place. Two psychics had been invited to visit Trapper's land to determine who remains there. Is it Trapper or some ancient Seminole spirits who constantly ask Cheryl, the ranger, for help? The boat ride to Trapper Nelson's site was an ethereal experience. A full moon reflected onto the dark waters of the Loxahatchee as the pontoon moved quietly on the water. Owls announced our approach with their distinctive hoots, and the cool October breeze accompanied us down the river as the captain dodged floating logs. The boat captain identified two yellow dots on the riverbank as alligator eyes. This trip is a way to experience Florida that should not be missed.

After tying up to Trapper's dock, we went toward the chickee, and the ranger built a fire for light. A seance was held at the site, and Pat Allen, a trance medium, said, "He's here. His spirit is very strong here. He was a strong person. He would never have taken his life. His brother killed him and tried to make it look like a suicide. He suffered, but he's okay; he's at peace. He's just here to make sure everything is fine. He's pleased with the park. He wants lots of people here. He wants you to fix something; I don't know what. There are two burial sites in here. They will be uncovered, but he wants them covered back up. He's going to direct someone to the sites so that no one disturbs the peace of the Indians ." Further into the seance, she said, "His spirit was just here, but he couldn't come all the way through. He wanted to come through." She repeated that he was at peace, and he walked the grounds because this was his paradise. "He used to sit here and talk to the great spirits. There are two Indian sites here. He doesn't want them disturbed, but he wants to let people know they are here. There's a tall Indian with two feathers who is still here." The psychic told me that Trapper would appear to me. That evening, he did not. However, as I was leaving the chickee, Trapper told me to come back when there weren't so many others there. I will go back.

VISITING THE SITE

This park is very popular for campers wanting to experience southern Florida in its natural state. There are two campgrounds in the park which offer different facilities, including primitive camping (tent area with portable toilets), cabins, and RV parking. Canoes can be rented, and there are nature trails and fresh- and saltwater fishing areas. A boat takes park visitors down the Loxahatchee to Trapper Nelson's place. Camping fees vary. The park's proximity to other visitor attractions, such as shopping, a dog track, Jupiter's beautiful beaches, and the Intracoastal Waterway, make it advisable to request reservations in advance. Information may be obtained by calling (407) 546-2771.

DIRECTIONS

This state park is on A1A just north of Jupiter. Signs designate the entrance. The river picnic area is approximately a five-mile drive from the main gate.

CORAL CASTLE IN HOMESTEAD

T*hirty miles south of Miami* lies a National Historic Site which has baffled engineers and visitors alike who come to see this unusual coral creation. Featured on the television programs "In Search Of," "That's Incredible," and "Mysterious Places," it is Florida's Stonehenge. The unanswered question of Coral Castle is how a small man, weighing barely one hundred pounds, could extract coral from the earth in giant hunks and carve his castle and furniture from chunks weighing tons. It would be difficult to do with modern machinery, but Edward Leedskalnin did it with simple tools over a thirty-year period.

Leedskalnin came to Florida from the tiny Baltic country of Latvia, where he had lost the love of his beautiful "Sweet Sixteen," as he referred to her. His efforts were a monument to that love. When he first came to Florida, he lived at Florida City, where he built most of the coral furniture. Later he moved to the ten-acre plot on U.S. 1

where the present Coral Castle is located. Here he built a two-story tower house containing 235 tons of coral. By himself, with his simple tools, he put in place blocks that weighed four to six tons each. His coral rock furniture is unbelievable. It is a collection of carved and perfectly balanced couches, tables, chairs, and fountains. One table is shaped like the state of Florida, with a carved-out area for Lake Okeechobee. This table alone weighs three tons. His rocking chairs weigh tons, yet they rock at the touch of a finger. Leedskalnin carved a spiral staircase leading to his underground stone refrigerator. A heart-shaped table has flowers growing from an opening in the middle.

Leedskalnin used a pillar that weighs twenty-three tons as a telescope. A small hole is carved through it. Near that he erected another piece of coral and bored a small hole in it also. There are no lenses in the telescope, but cross wires allowed him to focus accurately on the North Star. His fascination with astronomy is evident from the carvings that top the back wall of his home: a Crescent of the East, a Saturn, and Mars. Saturn is eighteen tons of coral, including the ring.

A wall eight feet high and three feet thick surrounds his castle. The tower itself, his living quarters, is reached by stone steps. It contains his bed and a chair, both suspended from the ceiling, and tables jutting out from the walls. Nothing rested on the floor to obstruct him when he cleaned his castle. The space below his living area was his workroom and storage area. Outside, with his furniture, is a bathtub and a mirror cleverly fashioned to provide a reflection.

The rear entrance to his castle was a nine-ton door, perfectly balanced in the coral opening with a half-inch clearance around it. It worked on a swivel which allowed it to be opened with only the touch of a finger.

Leedskalnin built his castle in secrecy, using the most basic tools: chains, levers, and pulleys. This system was built from discarded parts he had salvaged from junk yards. He boasted proudly that he had never ruined one piece of coral—an incredible feat considering how easily coral crumbles when it is worked.

Leedskalnin sculpted a huge chair from which he could watch the traffic pass on U.S. 1, above the wall. He sought no visitors, but would allow the curious to come in. He asked for donations only. His enter-

Wall at Coral Castle

tainment was mostly reading, especially scientific journals he found in the local library, which he reached by riding his bicycle. He lived a spartan life, brooding until his death for the loss of his Sweet Sixteen, who never came to him. He died in 1951 at the age of sixty-four.

An advertisement in the *Miami Daily News* placed by Leedskalnin read as follows: "Read about magnetic current, what it is, how it is made, what makes it, and the way it runs in the wire. Then you will know what the north and south pole individual magnets can do, and then you will know what electricity is. Send a dollar by return mail and you will get an eight-thousand-word booklet. Only those who want to experiment should order the booklet. The other people should save their money."

Edward Leedskalnin was known as an eccentric, and his lifestyle and writings back this up, but whatever else is said of him, he accomplished a feat with his Coral Castle that engineers cannot explain. He took his secret, and his love for the young Latvian girl, with him to the grave.

HAUNT HISTORY

Some who have seen Coral Castle believe Leedskalnin used levitation and supernatural powers to create his monumental work. Chris Borg is on the Board of Directors of Broward County's Archaeological Society, based in Dania, just south of Fort Lauderdale. He is the Chairman of "Psy Archaeology," a team of psychics working with a team of scientists. "To give you an idea of how accurate some of these people are, they are able to pinpoint exactly where things are and what they are, such as buried artifacts," Borg said. "I brought Leedskalnin through one night," Borg said. "I was able to say only a few sentences to him. I had to bring him through twice because of a disturbance, then I brought him through again and there was another disturbance and he was pulled away.

"It is said there are two distinct areas of energy at Coral Castle. Psychics go to Coral Castle because they're sensitive. By that I mean they can sense things. That energy, those vortexes, are so powerful that it opens up their own personal senses. I know that when I'm there, I'm much more acute. I have dowsed a number of places in there, and if you have a pendulum, it will work itself up to a horizontal position."

One of the employees at Coral Castle, Barbara Agramonte, said she had heard of strange things, mostly from visitors who came through. She particularly remembered a Seminole visitor who took pictures: after having them developed, he noticed figures in the pictures that were not there when he took the photos.

VISITING THE SITE

Coral Castle is open from 9:00 A.M. to 6:00 P.M. daily. It closes on Thanksgiving Day at 3:00 P.M. and is closed on Christmas Day. Admission is $6.50, but discount coupons are can be found in tourist booklets, which are available at area convenience stores. Phone (305) 248-6344.

DIRECTIONS

From the west coast of Florida, take I-75 to Rt. 997 (U.S. 27). Go south to SW 288th Street. Turn left and go one mile to U.S. 1. Coral Castle is across the street. From the northeast coast of Florida, take

Coral Chair at Coral Castle

Exit 6 from Turnpike Extension. Go left one mile to SW 288th Street and go right for two miles to SW 157th Avenue. Turn right and then turn into the parking lot. From the Keys, Take U.S. 1 to SW 286th Street.

BILTMORE HOTEL IN CORAL GABLES

The *Biltmore, which turned seventy* years old in January 1996, wears her age proudly and well. The Biltmore is a historic hotel in Coral Gables, and its guest log is a register of the rich and famous. Walking on the terraces around the pool, the visitor is shaded from the Florida sun by bougainvillea, which smiling workers tuck up into the lattice overhead. Located only four miles south of Miami International Airport and a scant five miles from downtown Miami, the Biltmore, with its charm and sophistication, has endowed Coral Gables with an architectural landmark consistent with the Mediterranean-Revivalist style of homes in the surrounding area.

Visitors are greeted with an arched driveway that leads to an impressive entrance: tall columns, a Spanish-style red tile roof, hand-painted ceilings, marble floors, and carved woodwork. The hotel has 275 guest rooms, including suites and tower suites. It is now under the management of Westin Hotels and Resorts, under a lease with the city of Coral Gables. George E. Merrick, who developed the Coral Gables area and founded the University of Miami, joined with hotel magnate John Bowman at the height of the Florida land boom to build a hotel that "would serve as a center of sports and fashion." His intentions are being carried out again, although it served as a Veterans Administration hospital to serve the wounded at the onset of World War II. During that time, many windows were sealed with concrete, and government-issue linoleum covered the shiny marble floors. It also served as the early site of the University of Miami's School of Medicine. Ownership was conveyed to the city of Coral Gables by the federal government through the Historic Monuments Act and Legacy of Parks program in the early 1970s. It remained unoccupied for almost ten years. Then, in 1983, the city spent $47 million to restore it as a hotel. On December 31, 1987, a black-tie affair celebrated the hotel's reopening, but the celebration was short-lived. It closed again in 1990 due to financial difficulties.

In June of 1992, after $3 million had been spent to restore the eighteen-hole championship golf course, repair the pool, install state-of-the-art exercise equipment, and completely renovate the guest rooms, the Biltmore reopened with master chefs, round-the-clock concierge and room service, a private wine club, and every amenity available at any luxury resort throughout the world. Three ballrooms and twenty-four private meeting rooms cater to clientele for weddings or world gatherings. The three-hundred-foot copper-clad tower was copied from the Giralda Tower in Seville, Spain. The hotel pool is the largest one in the continental United States, measuring nearly twenty-two thousand square feet and holding six hundred thousand gallons of water. The hotel appeals to opulence and history on a scale unsurpassed in Florida.

In 1994 President Clinton opened the Summit of the Americas at the Biltmore, and in 1995 Lady Margaret Thatcher signed the papers inaugurating the Thatcher School of Democracy in one of the Biltmore's ballrooms. Several motion pictures have been filmed on the property, among them *Bad Boys*, *Fair Game*, and *The Specialist*. In the 1920s there were flappers and gangster soirées, beauty pageants, and aquatic shows featuring Esther Williams. Today, fashion models and brides pose by the gothic columns to take their place in history beside the Duke and Duchess of Windsor, Ginger Rogers, Judy Garland, Bing Crosby, Al Capone, the Roosevelts, and the Vanderbilts.

HAUNT HISTORY

The ghost of Thomas "Fatty" Walsh has been known to open doors for waitresses with trays in their hands. Lamp shades are stolen, and messages are written on steamy mirrors. In 1979 a group of Science Fiction Club members went to the Biltmore when it was vacant. They took tape recorders and recorded, they thought, nothing but their own clomping around from room to room as they poked around in the deserted building looking for anything odd. It was only when they got home, tired and disappointed at not encountering anything, that they heard the sound on their tapes. The sound "shocked us," said Barbara Clipper, the society's president. "None of us heard it while we were there, and we didn't expect it on the tape. It can't be any of us

Biltmore Hotel

and it can't be any animals." The sound was unexplained heavy breathing, lasting for about a minute, ending with what sounded like a resolved sigh. Because so many traumas have happened within the walls of the building, there are many presences, and historians and writers have tried, throughout the Biltmore's seventy years, to sort out the reasons for the energies that remain in the hotel.

Thomas "Fatty" Walsh left New York in 1928, accompanied by a friend and fellow mobster, Arthur Clark. Fatty Walsh left to avoid the incessant questioning by New York police about the death of another mobster friend. He came to Florida looking for a new life and rented an apartment in Coral Gables. There, Edward Wilson, a gambler who knew Fatty, told Fatty that he had leased the thirteenth and fourteenth floors of the Biltmore tower, and in his penthouse was operating a speakeasy of sorts, where wealthy Miamians came for gambling and bootlegged liquor. Wilson and Fatty became partners in the operation, but the partnership soon wore thin, and in March 1929, with over one hundred people at the black-tie gaming tables, the two men were heard arguing. Suddenly, Wilson pulled a gun from his jacket and shot Fatty with two bullets. Fatty's friend, Clark, rushed to his side, and Wilson fired a shot at him also. Wilson then ran through the hall and somehow got to the lobby and into the parking lot. The guests, not wanting to become involved in something that might give them unfavorable headlines, crowded together for protection, but no one made an attempt to chase Wilson.

Sergeant Brasher and another patrolman who were on duty that night went to the Biltmore as soon as they heard of the shooting. They ran through the lobby and attempted to use the elevators to get to the penthouse. When they found them inoperable, they tried to use the stairwells, but they were locked. After what seemed like an eternity, the two policemen saw that finally the elevators were in operation. When they reached the tower rooms, all they found was Fatty lying dead next to his friend, Clark, who was wounded by the single shot he had taken from Wilson's gun. No sign of the gaming tables and bootlegged liquor remained. Nothing about the furnishings or carpet could ever prove anyone was in the room before the murder.

It has been rumored that the Dade County District Attorney's Office, later called the State Attorney's Office, put Wilson aboard a plane to Havana, which indicates that law enforcement agencies were profiting from the gambling operation. Police lost track of Clark after he left the hospital. In 1946, the Los Angeles police said they were checking a story for the Federal Bureau of Investigation that a man named Wilson had confessed to being connected to the murder of Fatty Walsh. When the Los Angeles police asked for the records of that crime, they were told there were none. This fact tends to back up the rumors that the law was somehow involved in the Biltmore gambling site.

In 1978, mediums and parapsychologists were taken to the Biltmore for a seance. None of them were told of the circumstances surrounding their visit. Some of the psychics picked up vibrations in various places, but all insisted there was something unusual about the elevators. Psychic Anne Phillips said, "There was a lot of commotion here." Then the psychics took each flight of stairs, continuing to the thirteenth floor, where they insisted something had happened in the past. They continued to the balcony, and went to a room at the southeast corner. All of them explained that they had felt four people follow them up the stairs, and that the four did not like this room. Hayes, a member of the group, said, "I can feel the energy!" Another member said that she felt there was a lot of drinking and partying in that room. Anne Phillips, who had first said the elevators were a part of the drama, now said there was a little old man with a cane. Then the group agreed that whatever had happened took place down by the fireplace on the thirteenth floor and that whoever had followed them up the stairs had not actively participated in the traumatic event. They said numbers were involved with whatever had taken place on the thirteenth and fourteenth floors. The group said there was some kind of warning and then a lot of fast action. They also said the police were involved but in a superficial way. At one point, Phillips said, "He's making me nervous, the little old man with the cane."

A tapping noise was heard when the tape of the subsequent seance was later transcribed. The tapping got very loud, almost drowning out the conversation of the psychics. After the seance, all participants agreed that there were possibly hundreds of entities in the room. William Guerrant Kimbrough, the retired chief of the Coral Gables Police department, was interviewed at his home after the psychics visited the Biltmore. He confirmed that indeed there was information on the tapes brought out during the seance that was never published in the papers, such as the elevators being out of working order. He was the other patrolman who, with Sergeant Brasher, had investigated the shootings that evening in 1929 at the Biltmore penthouse.

The Biltmore Hotel has been the scene of many tragedies. Which of the spirits that once inhabited the building are still at the Biltmore? Are there wounded warriors from its days as a military hospital? Are there mobsters from the Roaring Twenties' days of prohibition? Are there wealthy socialites who spent their happiest years in the tower casino and bar? Although the hotel was closed during the 1970s, locals, it is said, made themselves comfortable on the golf course and witnessed the ghostly lights and sounds coming from the inside.

VISITING THE SITE

Tours of the Biltmore, hosted by the Dade Heritage Trust, are held every Sunday for hotel guests and local visitors. The hotel's rich history comes alive every Thursday at 7:00 P.M. by the lobby fireplace, where Miami Storytellers step back in time to the twenties and thirties, and tell of grand dames and mysterious ghosts which roam the tower suites.

With room rates from $159 to $1800 for suites, the Biltmore is not a casual stopover for the Florida sightseer. However, the Donald Ross golf course is open to the public; the fee is $26 per person with an additional $12.50 for cart rental. The poolside grill and pasta station are open to the public for lunch. This is not the usual poolside café with suntan-lotioned lounges, but rather a peaceful, shaded veranda for a relaxed lunch. Orchids decorate each table. The sound of water from fountains continuously replenishing the pool, combined with the sway of palm fronds, took us from the bustling Miami traffic to an oasis of pure enjoyment. The menu is varied and tasty. A Greek salad with a glass of wine was served by willing and friendly waiters. Parking is to the right of the hotel. For information about the tour or storytelling, call (305) 445-1926 or (800) 727-1926.

DIRECTIONS

From 826 (Palmetto Expressway), go east on Bird Avenue (S.W. 40th Street). Make a sharp left onto Granada off Bird, and turn left again on Anastasia. Left on Anastasia is the Biltmore.

ARTIST HOUSE IN KEY WEST

Opening the wrought-iron gate admits the visitor onto a cool shaded walkway, a welcome relief from the heat of the Key West summer. The Artist House stands as a modest example of Queen Anne architecture. Built in 1887 by Thomas Otto, a surgeon in Key West, the house passed later to his son, Eugene, who lived in it with his wife, Anne, and their two children, Robert and Mispha. Gene and Anne led a lavish lifestyle, entertaining frequently in the Eaton Street house. She was an accomplished concert pianist, and he was a well-known artist when they met in France. A picture of Anne hangs in one of the rooms, and a constant reminder of her spirit is evoked when strange things happen in and around the guest house.

HAUNT HISTORY

Linda, the housekeeper at Artist House, talked to me about what she had seen and experienced. "The ghost here is Anne Otto. I believe in God, so I believe in spirits. I'm not afraid of Anne—she's a good spirit. Gene beat his wife. She is buried elsewhere, not with her husband. Strange things happen here. Shutters open and close with no wind. Doors open ahead of you. But nothing bad happens, and I've gotten used to it.

"There was a doll here, a replica of Robert. A woman gave it to him when he was a child. Robert always blamed the doll when he did something wrong. One of the previous owners gave the doll to a museum. That's when Anne came back, as a spirit, to this house."

She told me more about the doll, showing me pictures that the owner had taken. When the doll was still at the residence, visitors were known to have heard it giggling. It was sometimes found in unexpected places, away from where it had been put down. It now is displayed in a case at the East Martello Museum.

Because Robert, the doll estimated to be almost one hundred years old, spent most of its time in the attic of the house, it is believed its presence is felt more there. Anne, though, has made herself known in the turret room and in other areas in the guest house.

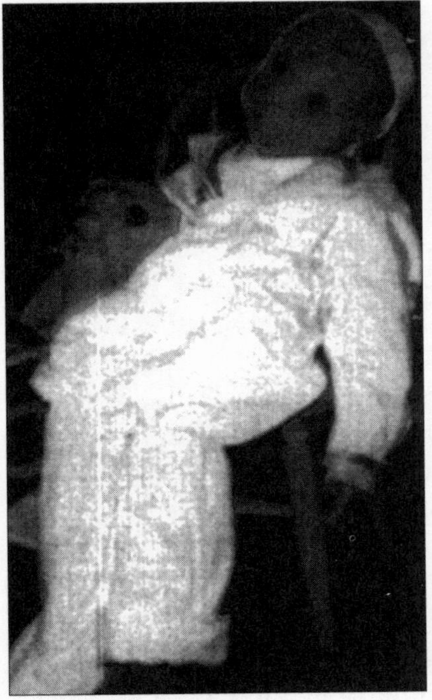

Robert

VISITING THE SITE

The rear courtyard holds a botanical Jacuzzi garden. Phone (800) 593-7898. It is well worth the trip to see the doll at the East Martello Museum. Phone (305) 296-3913. Robert is an unusual doll, with an unforgettable aura. The doll seems forlorn, as if waiting for something, and has strange effects on people who see him.

DIRECTIONS

Just off Duval Street, Artist House is easy to locate in Key West. The East Martello Museum is located at 3501 South Roosevelt Boulevard in Key West.

COLOURS IN KEY WEST

O*nly one half block from Duval Street* in Key West, in the heart of Old Town, sits a Victorian mansion that has been converted to a lovely guest house. From one of the upstairs guest rooms, the Key West scene plays out below the balcony. The island of Key West, which could be accessed only by boat before the 1900s, is dotted with houses that reflect many cultures. Colours—with its open porch, ceiling fans, and carved balustrade—is an example of the houses constructed when Key West was home to fortune-seeking wreckers (sea wreck salvagers) and cigar makers. In 1888 the city directory made note of the fact that "Key West pays nineteen-twentieths of the internal revenue collected in the state of Florida, which is largely due to . . . cigar manufacturing." One of these prominent manufacturers, Cuban Francisco Marrero, built his home at 410 Fleming Street with profits from the cigar industry.

Marrero was imprisoned in Cuba during that country's insurrection in 1869. He escaped and traveled to New York City, where he got a job in a cigar factory. After learning the entire process of manufacturing and marketing cigars, he became interested in Key West , having heard from shippers about Florida's island city and its cigar industry. Marrero subsequently moved to Key West and built a huge warehouse and forty-five cottages for the cigar makers. Revenue from the cigar industry as well as from his tenants increased his already substantial estate.

In 1886, the Great Fire, as it is known in Key West , lasted twelve hours and totally destroyed the island. Because of the isolation of the keys, insurers would not insure the wooden houses, which had no water source except cisterns that might dry out at any time. All of the warehouses and stores burned, and thousands of residents were left homeless. The property on which Colours now stands was in the section where the fire began.

Marrero bought the now-vacant lot and built the house on Fleming Street sometime between 1889 and 1890. The large, rectangular house, with its veranda and twin gables, stands out even in Key

West. The interior is now divided into guest rooms with private baths, an office, and a common area. The outdoor area centers mainly around the pool, which is surrounded by palms, jasmine, and bougainvillea. Colorful finches dominate one shaded corner, their colors and carefree attitude reflecting the very feeling of Key West.

Francisco Marrero died in Cuba in 1891, while he was on a trip to buy tobacco. He left a wife, Henriqueta, and eight children. Francisco had married Henriqueta in Key West on June 23, 1883. Six months after his death, Maria Ignacia de Marrero came to lay claim to his estate, disinheriting Henriqueta and her eight children. According to courthouse records, Maria was Francisco's first and only lawful wife and was therefore entitled to all of his estate. Francisco and Henriqueta's eight children were moved out of the house and left with no income from the sizable estate.

HAUNT HISTORY

"Show us the ghost, Michael," we entreated the handsome young house manager. He left his duties and freely talked to us about his experiences since he had been employed in the guest house. "Well, you all don't seem to have any negativity, so I don't think she'll be around. She makes herself known when there's negativity in the house. Usually what happens, people come in and they already have this feeling. Every once in a while the chandelier will dim intermittently. I always thought it was just a power surge.

"About a year ago, some people who had a reservation didn't let us know they would be late arriving until after ten P.M. Our office is open from eight in the morning until ten at night. They left a really nasty message on the machine. They said, 'We'll see you in the morning. We want our money back.' We didn't quite understand the whole message. We played it back four or five times. They showed up about eleven A.M. that next day. They were Spanish women. One had a very heavy Spanish accent, so we conversed in Spanish. We told her we would upgrade their reservation to a better room with a TV and such, and we bent over backwards to make her happy. She kept saying every room was too dark. She said it was creepy. The manager and my other housekeeper were here at the time. At that point, three doors upstairs slammed closed—one right after the other. We all looked up and saw

Colours

a shadow, and thought, Well, the wind did it. The two ladies decided they weren't going to stay. It happens like that every now and then. Two gentlemen in one room had a big argument. I was called out at three A.M. and had to make one of the gentlemen leave. Again, strange things happened, with the lights dimming and doors slamming.

"Once, two women were staying in the last room. I didn't meet them the night they checked in, but when I arrived the next morning, the first thing they said was, 'What kind of electrical connections do you have on this wall?' I said, 'Well, I have fuse boxes, and this and that,' and explained to them. They said, 'Well, there's something in the house; there are children in the house. There's some energy. We were up until three A.M. trying to direct the energy to move on.' They said there was so much energy that there was no end to it. They were perceptive about what was going on. They loved what had happened the night before and were so happy they had been here to experience it.

"On my very first day working here, I was doing some yard work out near the pool and I saw something at the kitchen door. I stopped what I was doing to go introduce myself to who I thought at first was another employee. I went to the door and walked all around the house. There was no one around. So I went back to finish what I was doing, and then I saw the figure of a small child by the Pepsi machine. This was in broad daylight. So I went nearer, and there was nothing. The next day I asked my manager, 'What is in the house?' He said, 'Are you psychic?' I said 'No—no.' Then he gave me the whole history. When the owner of the house died, his wife, Henriqueta, inherited the house. Six months later, Maria, his first wife, showed up. According to the law in those times, the house went to the first wife, and Henriqueta and her eight kids got thrown out. The second wife, Henriqueta, is the presence who is here. She always thought it was her house, and she returned. There is no history of what happened to her after she left here. But four or five of the kids are buried in the cemetery."

My sister, a confirmed skeptic who only came along to help with the camera and tape recorder, was standing next to me, listening to Michael. She said, "I was standing here listening to this, and out of the corner of my eye, I saw the upstairs window curtain blowing. Look at that curtain."

Michael said that although there were a few doors open upstairs into the hallway, that window was not open. My other sister then said she felt a cool draft come down the stairwell, right toward us. The upstairs window curtain, my sister insisted, had blown out from the window and halfway across the stairs. How could that happen if there was no wind and the window was closed?

Michael shrugged and smiled, as if to say these things were nothing new to him. He then gave us a tour of the house. He showed us the common area and pool, then showed us where he had been standing when he saw the figure in the doorway and later the child's figure by the soda machine. He also showed us pieces of broken tureens, toothbrushes made of bone, and other artifacts that had been found when the pool was excavated. Two upstairs rooms which are now divided were Henriqueta's quarters. Two men had once stayed there, Michael said. One of them began sleepwalking. His friend tried to wake him up. As he was walking toward Henriqueta's other room, the sleepwalker bumped into the wall. He said, "I'm following her. I was told to follow her."

Michael continued, "At night, I turn down the beds and put a mint on each pillow. Sometimes, in unoccupied rooms, I find things different than I've left them. Sometimes I can just feel something in the rooms. Just recently I was cleaning in one of the bathrooms. The house was empty, except for Eduardo and myself, and he was making the bed in the next room. I heard the cellular phone ring. You can call room to room, but not outside. I thought it was Eduardo, but he said he hadn't called. Also, we've had many instances of lights going on up in the attic. You need a long ladder to get up to the opening to the attic. People from across the street will call and tell me, 'You left your attic light on.' And we haven't been up there in a long time.

"Last year, I was in the house by myself, downstairs in the basement. No rooms were rented. I was getting supplies, and as I was going through stuff, I heard a voice say, 'Michael.' I turned around, and again I heard, 'Michael.' So I left and ran up the steps. I told the housekeeper about it, and she said, 'Oh, that happened to Eduardo.'"

At one time the guest house had been a restaurant. Michael offered that maybe Henriqueta was angry because of this. Also, he added that the operator of the tour train that passed through used to make mention of "Hettie," which was a nickname for Henriqueta; she may not have liked being referred to as Hettie. Most people who have experienced the ghost, however, believe that Henriqueta has obstinately refused to give up ownership of the old house, and that the spirits of her evicted children remain with her.

VISITING THE SITE

Rooms rent from December 15th to April 1st and cost from $110 to $185. During the summer, rates are $80 to $135. This includes a continental breakfast. The swimming pool at the rear of the guesthouse is "clothing optional."

DIRECTIONS

Colours Guest House is at 410 Fleming Street, in the heart of Old Town, a short walk from Duval Street. Phone (305) 532-9341 or (800) ARRIVAL.

FORT ZACHARY TAYLOR IN KEY WEST

B*ecause this fort has the largest collection* of Civil War cannons in the United States, Fort Taylor was placed on the National Register of Historic Places in 1971. It is now designated as a National Historic Landmark.

Construction began on the fort shortly after Florida became a state. In 1850, the year President Taylor died in office, the fort was given its present name. It was completed in 1866, twenty-one years after construction began. Hurricanes and yellow fever took their toll on the men laboring to complete it. The finished fort was three stories high, had sanitary facilities flushed by the tides, and included a desalination plant.

Fort Taylor was used during the Spanish-American War, and then in 1889 the top level was removed to install more modern weapons. Radar eventually replaced the weapons, and in 1947 the Army turned the fort over to the Navy. During the Civil War, the fort was in Union hands, and it became an important line of defense. The cannons used then had a range of three miles, which effectively prevented the Confederate Navy from taking the island of Key West.

Howard England, who was stationed at Naval Air Station in Key West in the 1970s, began digging around the abandoned old fort out of curiosity. He uncovered Civil War armaments that had been buried in the old gun rooms. The Civil War cannons were buried and used as fill to strengthen the fort's bastions before the Spanish-American War. In 1976, the state of Florida obtained ownership of the fort from the federal government, and the park was opened in 1985. A museum is located at the fort, with exhibits of artifacts and models of the guns and the original fort. The original Civil War cannons are displayed on the open grounds of the fort.

Today, the park is enjoyed by visitors to this southernmost part of the United States. The park itself is situated at the lowest end of Key West and provides a perfect spot to enjoy the Atlantic Ocean. A man-made reef extends into the ocean, providing a way for snorkelers to view a variety of beautiful fish without needing a boat. On the west side of the park is a designated fishing area.

HAUNT HISTORY

Howard England said that he used to lie awake at night, trying to figure out where the desalinization plant and other structures had been located. Then an apparition came to him. "It seemed to me one day I was in room thirteen. I heard a voice say, 'What be you looking for, sonny?'

"I looked up, and a man was standing next to me in a Civil War uniform, with a white beard." He told the soldier he was looking for old guns and things.

The bearded man said, "Well, it's here. That's old Betsy. That was my gun. This was my room."

The next day, England continued digging. Right where the spirit had told him to look, he found the first gun. The soldier visited England again and revealed his name—Wendell Gardiner. He also told him where the old desalinization plant had been. England never tried to trace the soldier's name, but one day he was chatting with a tourist about the fort, and the tourist offhandedly said, "One of my ancestors served at this fort. His name was Wendell Gardiner."

Volunteer Bud Eberly insisted he heard ghosts whistle, howl, and sing "Dixie." Frank Ofeldt, who is a ranger at another state park now, related his unusual experiences at Fort Zachary Taylor. "Some of the things that I have seen, people don't want to believe. I guess if you really believe as I did, growing up, then studying Civil War history—everything that I've seen and experienced, I knew was real. It was an interesting place to be. I'll never forget some of the things that happened to me while I was there. One time I saw a soldier right in front of my eyes. He was at the other end of the fort. He saw me, looked straight at me, then turned around and just disappeared. Other times I've seen soldiers lined up, all in a row, out of the corner of my eye.

"Another time I was in the fort by myself. I saw a shadow break the shafts of light of three places—first one, then the next, then the next. It was someone walking. It couldn't have come from outside. But there was no one in the fort. Something broke the sunlight all the way down. I've seen men walk back and forth, especially around the latrine area. I've seen figures walk down to the kitchen—the dining hall. Once, in the main gallery where the guns would be, I heard someone say, 'Attention'— a very faint voice. Cliff Rogers, another ranger, experienced some things down there. Of course, most people won't believe you.

"I didn't start seeing actual soldiers until I'd been there awhile. On July 7, I was in the fort doing some work. I heard all these doors shutting—slamming. So I went out to look around. It was dark, and I had no flashlight. I checked all the locks. Nothing was unlocked. That next night I was in there working again. I saw a Civil War soldier at the other end. He walked all the way down, turned, saw me—just looked at me—then turned back and walked away. I said 'OK, that's it, I'm out of here,' and I left. After that, I started seeing them more often. I talked with Howard, the archaeologist. He saw a Civil War soldier walk right through a wall. Many times I saw men in uniform, at a distance, but I'd never see them directly in front of me, except the one. That one—he looked right at me, and I looked at him. I was completely shocked. I found it was best not to say anything, just to experience things that happened. The best time to see them is just as the sun sets, or early in the morning.

"I've heard voices, and I've heard whistling. I couldn't make out exactly what they were saying. Sometimes items in the office would be moved and then put back later on. I think they only show themselves to certain people. They're there for a purpose. They never left. They're still serving their post. I've tried to go in with a camera and take their picture. They don't show up. If I just go in and do my work, then I see them."

Ofeldt ended our interview by saying that his feelings were very strong about these old forts, where men had died and been wounded, and that he wished all the visitors and their children would treat the forts with respect, as one would a battleground, like Flander's Field. He reminded me that Fort Zachary stands as a memorial to men who fought for a cause and gave their life for their beliefs.

VISITING THE SITE

This fort is at the southern end of Key West. Guided tours are available daily, and a museum at the site contains artifacts and models of the original guns. The park is a wonderful place for a family to picnic, snorkel, and swim after having seen the fort.

DIRECTIONS

The fort is easily located at the southern end of Southard Street, in Key West, on the Atlantic Ocean.

BIBLIOGRAPHY

REGION ONE: Northwest

DORR HOUSE IN PENSACOLA

Johnson, Sandra and Leora Sutton. *Ghosts, Legends and Folklore of Old Pensacola*. 1994. Available from Pensacola Historical Society, 117 East Government Street, Pensacola, FL 32502.

Johnson, Sandra. Interview with author. 12 August 1996.

"Welcome to the Dorr House." Available from Pensacola Heritage Foundation, 410 Florida Blanca Street, Pensacola, FL 32501.

LEAR HOUSE IN PENSACOLA

Johnson, Sandra, and Leora Sutton. *Ghosts Legends and Folklore of Old Pensacola*. 1994. Available from Pensacola Historical Society, 117 East Government Street, Pensacola, FL 32502.

Johnson, Sandra. Interview with author. 12 August 1996.

Powell, Gary, and Beverly Madison Currin. *The Search for the Lost Rectors: Archaeology and History of Old Christ Church*. Pensacola: University of West Florida, 1991.

"The Lear House." Available from Pensacola Historical Society, 117 East Government Street, Pensacola, FL 32502.

OLD CHRIST CHURCH IN PENSACOLA

Johnson, Sandra. Interview with author. 13 August 1996.

Powell, Gary, and Beverly Madison Currin. *The Search for the Lost Rectors - Archaeology and History of Old Christ Church*. Pensacola: University of West Florida, 1991.

Powell, Gary. Interview with author. 4 September 1996.

LIGHTHOUSE AT PENSACOLA BAY

Gannon, Michael. *The New History of Florida*. Gainesville: University Press of Florida, 1996.

Hallford, Scott. "Do You Believe There are Ghosts on NAS?" *Gosport* (Pensacola, FL) 26 October 1990: 17.

Henning, Ann. "NAS Hosts Ghostly Guardians." *Gosport* (Pensacola, FL) 29 October 1982.

Hu, Winnie. "Shedding Light on Mystery." *Pensacola News Journal*, 15 January 1995: 1E.

"Pensacola Lighthouse History." www.erols.com/lthouse/plt.htm

ARCADIA ARCHAEOLOGY PROJECT IN MILTON

Phillips, John. "The Arcadia Story." UWF Archaeology Institute site on the Internet (may be accessed with any common search engine).

Weekes, Warren. Interview with author. 14 August 1996.

SHELL MOUND AT CEDAR KEY

Ralls, Mark Allen. "The Ghost of Annie Simpson." *St. Petersburg Times Floridian*. 31 October 1982.

Roberts, Anna Raye. Interview with author. 1 November 1995.

ISLAND HOTEL IN CEDAR KEY

Sanders, Alison. Interview with author. 1 November 1995.

Sanders, Tom. *A Brief History of the Island Hotel*. February 1993. Available from The Island Hotel, P.O. Box 460, Cedar Key, FL 32625.

Sanders, Tom. Interview with author. 1 November 1995.

REGION TWO: Northeast

FORT CLINCH STATE PARK ON AMELIA ISLAND

Long, Phil. "Stories About Spirits Just Won't Die." *Miami Herald*, 29 October 1995: 8A.

Matthews, Tim. Interview with author. 4 April 1996.

TABBY HOUSE ON FORT GEORGE ISLAND

Dodge, Julia B. "An Island of the Sea," *Scribner's Magazine*, September 1877.

Florida State Parks: The Real Florida. Department of Environmental Protection, Division of Parks and Recreation: 12.

Webb, Terrence H. E. *Haunted Tabby House at Fort George Island*. Available from Jones Sand & Sea Shop, 9177 Heckscher Drive, Jacksonville, FL 32226.

KINGSLEY PLANTATION ON FORT GEORGE ISLAND

Duncan, Frances. Interview with author. 23 July 1996.

Gannon, Michael. *The New History of Florida*. Gainesville: University Press, 1996: 178.

Kingsley Plantation. Florida Department of Natural Resources, Division of Recreation and Parks. Available at the visitor's center.

CASTILLO de SAN MARCOS IN ST. AUGUSTINE

Gannon, Michael. *The New History of Florida*. Gainesville: University Press, 1996: 103.

Mills, Joe. Interview with author. 22 July 1996.

Windham, Kathryn Tucker. *Jeffrey Introduces 13 More Southern Ghosts*. Huntsville, AL: Strode, 1971.

ST. FRANCIS INN IN ST. AUGUSTINE

Harvey, Karen. "Eerie sights, sounds in old buildings." *The Compass*, 1 October 1992: 6.

Lonergan, Beverly. Interview with author. 3 April 1996.

46 AVENIDA MENENDEZ IN ST. AUGUSTINE

Harvey, Karen. "Phenomena." *The Compass*, 21 June 1990: 7.

Martini, Jim. Interview with author. 4 April 1996.

Navidi-O'Riordan, Cherie. *Site History of 46 Avenida Menendez*. 1993. Available at St. Augustine Historical Society, 271 Charlotte Street, St. Augustine, FL 32084.

LIGHTKEEPER'S HOUSE IN ST. AUGUSTINE
Harvey, Karen. "Phenomena." *The Compass*, 24 May 1990: 8.
Steward, Kathleen. Interview with author. 23 July 1996.
"The St. Augustine Lighthouse and Museum." http://staug.com/biz/lighthouse.htm.

DEVIL'S MILLHOPPER NEAR GAINESVILLE
Foster, Barbara. "Straight to the Devil." *Gainesville Sun*. 24 July 1977.
Long, Phil. "Stories About Spirits Just Won't Die." *Miami Herald*, 29 October 1995: 8A.

HERLONG MANSION IN MICANOPY
Anderson, Glenda. "Get a Glimpse of Florida's Past During Micanopy's Fall Festival." *News-Press* (Fort Myers, FL) 21 October 1990: 1G+.
Blackerby, Cheryl. "Quick Trips and Good Deals." *Atlanta Journal*, 2 October 1996.
Howard, Sonny. Interview with author. 16 October 1996.
Martin, Lydia. "Florida's Own Ghost Busters." *Miami Herald*, 31 October 1995: 1, 5E.

WASHINGTON OAKS STATE GARDENS NEAR ST. AUGUSTINE
A History of Washington Oaks State Gardens. Department of Environmental Protection. Available at the visitor's center.
Cheryl (Park Ranger). Interview with author. 22 July 1996.
Harvey, Karen. "Phenomena." *The Compass*, 21 June 1990: 7.
Long, Phil. "Stories About Spirits Just Won't Die." *Miami Herald*, 29 October 1995: 8A.

REGION THREE: Central East

DAYTONA PLAYHOUSE IN DAYTONA BEACH
Barnett, John S. Interview with author. 23 October 1995.
Hamburg, Jay. "The Dapper Ghost of the Daytona Playhouse."

Orlando Sentinel Florida Magazine, 26 October 1986: 1,12.

Koscoe, Kelly. Interview with author. 23 October 1995.

Peters, Jane. *Report on Playhouse Investigation*. 12 February 1986: 1+. Publication unavailable to the public.

Weigl, Chris. "Ghosts Find Daytona Beach Boo-tiful." *Daytona Beach Area News*, 30 October 1988: C1, 9.

WALDO'S MOUNTAIN IN VERO BEACH

Davis, Nancy. "Local Residents Recall Ghostly Experiences." *Vero Beach Press-Journal*, 31 October 1989: C1, 8.

Dilalla, Patricia. "Where's Waldo's Mountain?" *Vero Beach Press-Journal*, 6 June 1993.

MacGregor, Rob, and Trish Janeshutz. "Waldo's Mountain." *Omni*, August 1988: 75.

Martin, Judy. Interview with author. 24 October 1995.

ASHLEY'S IN ROCKLEDGE

"Brutally Murdered Body of Cocoa Girl is Found Yesterday." *Cocoa Tribune*, 22 November 1934.

Cox, Billy. "Lingering Guests." *Florida Today*, 4-8 July 1982: 1E+, 1D+.

Denemark, Malcolm. "I Saw No One." *Florida Today*, 7 July 1982.

Grant, Kathy. Interview with author. 24 October 1995.

Klinkenberg, Jeff. "Spirits in the Night." *St. Petersburg Times*, 10 September 1986: 1+.

CASSADAGA NEAR DAYTONA

Cassadaga Spiritualist Camp. Southern Cassadaga Spiritualist Camp Meeting Association. Available at Cassadaga Camp Bookstore and Information Center.

Henderson, Janie. *The Story of Cassadaga*. Cassadaga, FL: Pisces, 1992.

Langley, Liz. "A Haunting We Will Go." *Orlando Sentinel*, 27 October 1991: 14.

REGION FOUR: Central

MAITLAND ART CENTER

Johnson, Dean, and Laura Stewart. "Nice Place for a Haunting." *Orlando Sentinel Florida Magazine*, 28 October 1984: 10, 16.

Maitland Art Center. Available in the lobby of the gallery.

POLASEK GALLERIES IN WINTER PARK

Moran, Margaret. Interview with author. 24 October 1997.

Shutt, Henrietta P. *Albin Polasek*. Available at Polasek Galleries, 633 Osceola Avenue, Winter Park, FL 32789.

INSIDE-OUTSIDE HOUSE IN LONGWOOD

Descriptive Notes, Old Longwood "Village" Walking Tour. Available at Central Florida Historical Society, P.O. Box 520500, Longwood, FL 32752-0500.

Inside-Outside House. Available at Central Florida Historical Society, P.O. Box 520500, Longwood, FL 32752-0500.

McLeod, Betty Jo. *This Month at Browser's Barn*. October 1984. Available at Central Florida Historical Society, P.O. Box 520500, Longwood, FL 32752-0500.

Redditt, Pamm. Interview with author. 24 October 1997.

REGION FIVE: Central West

FORT COOPER STATE PARK NEAR INVERNESS

Craig, Lea. Interview with author. 30 October 1996.

Eden, John H. *Fort Cooper, the Gallant Defense of a Perilous Position*. 1 October 1977. Available at Fort Cooper Ranger Station.

Yosik, Steve. Interview with author. 22 October 1996.

TAMPA THEATER

Art of Tampa. Arts Council of Hillsborough County. Available from Arts Council of Hillsborough County, 725 East Kennedy Boulevard, Room 401, Tampa, FL 33602.

Brill, Noni. "Inside Downtown Tampa." *Tampa Tribune*, June 1994.

Grimes, Sandra. "A Ghost Story." *Tampa Tribune*, 19 February 1982: C1+.

Hall, H. Kevin. "Does Late Worker's Ghost Haunt Theater?" *Tampa Tribune*, 16 June 1983: A6+.

Koenig, John. "Best of Tampa." *America West*, October 1994.

Norman, Michael, and Beth Scott. "The Vestigial Projectionist." *Haunted America*, New York: TOR, 1995.

Otto, Steve. "Old Theater is a Balcony to the Stars." *Tampa Tribune*, 29 October 1993.

Schroeder, Tara. Interview with author. 28 November 1995.

Vogel, Chris. "Check Out These Local Haunts for Tales of the Supernatural." *Tampa Tribune* Baylife, 31 October 1995.

Warren, Bill. "Phantom of the Tampa Theater." *Tampa Tribune*, 28 September 1978.

CENTER PLACE IN BRANDON

Ames, Arnold. "She Haunts the Cultural Center, Or Does She?" *Tampa Tribune*, 6 September 1982: EH1.

Center Sounds. Bimonthly flyer published by and available at Center Place. July/August 1995.

Greater Brandon Area Demographic Information. Greater Brandon Chamber of Commerce. Available from Greater Brandon Chamber of Commerce, 808 Oakfield Drive, Brandon, FL 33511.

Rodriguez, Lisa W. "The History of Brandon." *Community Connections*, 2 August 1990: 1+.

Ruth, Gale. Interview with author. 11 October 1995.

JOHNS PASS AT TREASURE ISLAND

Beard, Bruce. "Spirits of the Whitus Brothers Still Haunt the Waterfront." *St. Petersburg Times Magazine*, 19 June 1966: 8.

Miller, Betty Jean. "Pinellas Past & Present." *St. Petersburg Times*, 14 October 1991.

REGION SIX: Southwest

BOCA GRANDE LIGHTHOUSE ON GASPARILLA ISLAND

Cohorn, Michael. Interview with author. 31 August 1996.

"History of Boca Grande." *Boca Beacon 1996 Visitor's Guide*: 15+.

Porter, Dave. Interview with author. 31 August 1996.

CABBAGE KEY INN

Natale, Judy. Interview with author. 30 August 1996.

Sylvain, Rick. "A Leaf From the Past." *St. Petersburg Times*, 16 April 1995: 6E.

PALM COTTAGE IN NAPLES

Palm Cottage. Collier County Historical Society. Available from Palm Cottage, 137 12th Avenue South, Naples, FL 33939.

Ryan, Fritzi. Interview with author. 15 October 1997.

REGION SEVEN: Southwest

JONATHAN DICKINSON STATE PARK (TRAPPER NELSON) NEAR JUPITER

Allen, Pat. Spiritualist at seance. 26 October 1996.

Breunig, Myra. Spiritualist at seance. 26 October 1996.

DuBois, Bessie Wilson. *The History of the Loxahatchee River*. 1981. Available from Florida History Center and Museum, 805 North U.S. Highway One, Jupiter, FL 33477.

Jonathan Dickinson State Park. Florida Department of Environmental Protection, Division of Recreation and Parks. Available at main gate to park.

Long, Phil. "Stories About Spirits Just Won't Die." *Miami Herald*, 29 October 1995: 8A.

Wells, Cheryl. Interview with author. 25 September 1996.

CORAL CASTLE IN HOMESTEAD

Agramonte, Barbara. Interview with author. 19 June 1996.

Borg, Chris. Interview with author. 26 July 1996.

Kofoed, William. "Wizard of Coral Castle." *Coronet*, February 1958: 103.

MacGregor, Rob, and Trish Janeshutz. "Coral Castle: 30 Years' Work." *Omni*, August 1988: 75.

Paulson, Judith. *On Coral Castle*. www.m-m.org/jz/sphinxr.html

BILTMORE HOTEL IN CORAL GABLES

Curry, Ginger Simpson. "Keeping Spirits Up." *Floridian*, 14 February 1982: 12, 13, 15, 18.

Gehrke, Donna. "Biltmore Hotel offers some ghostly delights." *Miami Herald*, 30 October 1994.

Matsuda, Craig. "They seek phantom of the Biltmore." *Miami Herald*, 28 October 1979.

Winer, Richard, and Nancy Osborn. *Haunted Houses*. New York: Bantam, July 1979: 171+.

ARTIST HOUSE IN KEY WEST

Caemmerer, Alex. *The Houses of Key West*. Sarasota: Pineapple Press, 1992, 99.

Gordon, Marsha, "A Halloween Guide" *Island Life*, 27 October 1988: 4+.

Linda. Interview with author. 21 June 1996.

Miller. Interview with author. 21 June 1996.

COLOURS IN KEY WEST

Barron, Michael. Interview with author. 21 June 1996.

Gordon, Marsha. "A Halloween Guide." *Island Life*, 27 October 1988: 4+.

Wells, Sharon "Key West—A Brief Chronicle." December 1977.

FORT ZACHARY TAYLOR IN KEY WEST

Fort Zachary Taylor State Historic Site. Available from Southeast Publications USA Incorporated, 4360 Peters Road, Ft. Lauderdale, FL 33317.

Long, Phil. "Stories About Spirits Just Won't Die." *Miami Herald*, 29 October 1995: 8A.

Ofeldt, Frank. Interview with author. 24 July 1996.

INDEX